A NEW AND GLORIOUS LIFE

Also by Michelle Herman

❋

Missing

A NEW AND GLORIOUS LIFE

NOVELLAS

Michelle Herman

Carnegie Mellon University Press
Pittsburgh, 1998

Acknowledgments

"Hope Among Men" first appeared in *The Northwest Review*, "Auslander" in *Twenty Under Thirty: Best Stories by America's New Young Writers*.

❂

Debts of gratitude are owed to the Department of English and the College of Humanities of the Ohio State University, the Ohio Arts Council, the MacDowell Colony, and Yaddo; to my brother, Scott Herman, who leapt to my aid at a crucial juncture; to M.V. Clayton, Kathy Fagan, Marlene Kocan, Marilyn Schwartz, Marian Young, Sharon Dilworth, Christopher Griffin, Lore Segal, Lee K. Abbott, the brilliant and generous Nancy Zafris, and the gifted, intrepid MFA students at Ohio State; and especially to my husband, Glen Holland, who forbore—who continues to forbear (whose forbearance, indeed, is legion)—his own work every morning for the sake of mine.

❂

Acknowledgment is made to Heather McHugh for the use of her poem "To Have To" from *Hinge and Sign*, published by Wesleyan University Press.

Library of Congress Card Catalog Number 97-077970
ISBN 0-88748-284-8 Pbk.
Printed and Bound in the United States of America
10 9 8 7 6 5 4 3 2 1

Contents

For Vicki

AUSLANDER

The translator, Auslander, was at first flattered. She listened, astonished, for a full minute before the caller— Rumanian, she had guessed after his initial words of praise— paused for a breath, allowing her the opportunity to thank him.

"No, no," he said. "It is I who should thank you, and furthermore apologize for disturbing you at your home. Naturally I am aware that this was most presumptuous. I admit I hesitated a long while before I placed the call. Still, it was difficult to resist. When I read the contributors' notes and discovered that you 'lived and worked in New York City,' I felt it was a great stroke of luck. I must tell you I was surprised that your telephone number was so easily obtained from Directory Assistance."

Auslander laughed. "I've never found it necessary to keep the number a secret. I'm not exactly in the position of getting besieged with calls from admiring readers."

"You are far too modest," the Rumanian said. He spoke hoarsely but with a certain delicacy, as if he were whispering. "Your essay was truly quite something. Such insight! Your understanding of the process of translating poetry is complete, total."

"It's kind of you to say so," Auslander said. She had begun to shiver. The telephone call had caught her just as she was preparing to lower herself into the bathtub, and she wished she had thought to grab a towel when she'd rushed to answer the phone.

"I assure you I am not being kind," he said. "Your work impressed me greatly. It is so difficult to write of such matters with cleverness and charm as well as intelligence. I imagine you are a poet yourself?"

"No, not actually," Auslander said. Her teeth were chattering now. "Could you possibly hold on for just a second?" She set the receiver down and clambered over the bed to shut the window. Across the small courtyard a man sat at his kitchen table laying out a hand of solitaire. He looked up at Auslander and she stared back for an instant before she remembered that she was naked. As she yanked down the bamboo shade, the man raised his hand in slow expressionless salute.

"Oh, I fear I *have* interrupted you," the Rumanian said when she returned to the phone.

"Not at all." Auslander cradled the receiver on her shoulder as she dug through a heap of clothes on the floor. She extracted a flannel shirt and shrugged her arms into it. "Really, it was very good of you to call."

"Good of me? No, no, not in the least." He was nearly breathless. "Your essay was *outstanding*. Brilliant, I should say."

"My goodness," Auslander said. She sat down on the bed and buried her feet in the tangle of shirts and jeans and sweaters.

"Marvelous work. Profound. I do not exaggerate."

She was beginning to feel embarrassed. "You're much too kind," she murmured, and quickly, before he could protest again, she said, "Tell me, how did you happen to come across the essay?"

"Oh"—he laughed, a taut, high-pitched sound—"I read everything, everything. I haunt the periodical room of the library. Nothing is obscure to me. The literary quarterlies, the academic journals concerning literature, philosophy, history, religion— they all fascinate me, utterly. And I admit also that I have a particular interest in translation."

"A university library, it must be?"

"Ah, my God! How rude of me!" There was a soft thump; Auslander imagined him smacking his fist to his forehead. "I am so sorry. I have not properly introduced myself. My name is Petru Viorescu. I am a student—a graduate student—at Columbia University."

Auslander smiled into the phone. A Rumanian: she'd been right. "Well, Mr. Viorescu, I'm grateful for your compliments. It was very thoughtful of you to call."

This was greeted with silence. Auslander waited; he remained mute. She was just starting to become uneasy when he cleared his throat, and lowering his hushed voice still further said, "Miss Auslander, I do not want to appear in any way aggressive. Yet I wondered if it might be possible for us to meet."

"To meet?"

"Yes. You see, what I want to propose is a working meeting. Or, rather, a meeting to discuss the possibility . . .the possibility of working." He spoke quickly, with a nervous edge to his voice. "In your essay you wrote of the problems of translating some of the more diffuse, associative poetry in the Romance languages— of the light, respectful touch necessary for such work."

"Yes," she said. Cautious now.

"You have this touch, of course."

"I hope so," Auslander said.

"You even mentioned, specifically mentioned, a number of modern Rumanian poets. This was a great surprise and pleasure to me. I should add that I myself am Rumanian."

"Yes."

"Your biographical note included the information that you are fluent in nine languages. I assume, on the basis of your remarks in the second section of the essay, that my own is one."

"Your assumption is correct."

"And you are familiar with a great deal of Rumanian poetry."

"'A great deal,' I don't know about, Mr. Viorescu."

"You are feeling a little bit impatient with me now, yes?" He coughed out his odd laugh again. "Bear with me, please, for another moment. Have you in fact done any translation from the Rumanian as yet?"

Of course, Auslander thought. She struck her own forehead lightly with her palm. *A poet.* "Some," she said. A *student* poet yet. More than likely a very bad one. Unpublished, it went without saying. She sighed. Vanity! Only this had prevented her from assessing the matter sooner.

"I thought so. I would be most grateful if you would consider meeting with me to discuss a project I have in mind."

"I'm afraid I'm quite busy," Auslander said.

"I assure you I would not take up very much of your time. A half hour perhaps, no more."

"Yes, well, I'm afraid I can't spare even that."

"Please," he said. "It might be that ten or fifteen minutes would be sufficient."

Irritated, she said, "You realize, of course, that you haven't described the nature of this project."

"Oh, that is not possible at the moment." It occurred to her then that he actually *was* whispering. Always such drama with poets! "I do not mean to be secretive, believe me," he said. "It is only that I am unable to speak freely. But if you could spare a few minutes to see me . . ."

"I'm sorry," she said.

"Please."

It was not desperation—not exactly that—that she heard in this invocation. But surely, she thought, it was something akin to it. Urgency. Despair? Oh, nonsense, she told herself. She was being fanciful; she had proofread too many romance novels lately. With this thought came a pang of self-pity. She had lied when she'd said that she was busy. She had not had any real work since early fall; she had been getting by with freelance proofreading—drudgery, fools' work: romances and science fiction, houseplant care and rock star biographies. But that was beside the point, of course. Busy or not, she had every right to say no. She had refused such requests before, plenty of times. Those letters, so pathetic, forwarded to her by the journal or publisher to which they had been sent, asking her to translate a manuscript "on speculation"—they wrote letters that were like listings in *Writers' Market*, these young poets!—she had never had the slightest difficulty answering. But naturally it was easier to write a brief apologetic note than to disengage oneself politely on the phone. Still, it was only a matter of saying no, and saying it firmly so it would be clear the discussion was at an end.

Viorescu had fallen silent again. A manipulation, Auslander thought grimly. He was attempting to stir up guilt. And for what should she feel guilty? As if her sympathy were in the public domain! What did he think, did he imagine that publishing a scholarly essay in *Metaphrasis* meant she was a celebrity, someone with charity to spare?

"I'm assuming that your intent is to try to convince me to undertake the translation of a manuscript," she said. "First I must tell you that my services are quite expensive. Furthermore, you have read only a single essay which concerns approaches to translation and which tells you nothing whatsoever about my abilities as a translator."

"On the contrary," he said. "I have read two volumes of your translations, one from the Italian, one from the Portuguese, and a most remarkable group of poems in a quarterly, translated from the German. I apologize for not mentioning this earlier; I excuse myself by telling you I feared you would question my motives, the sincerity of my praise. So much flattery, you see. But I assure you I am entirely sincere. I have not been as thorough as I might have been in my research—my time is limited, you understand, by my own studies—but I am certain I have seen enough of your work to know that it is of the highest caliber. I am well aware that the finest poem can lose all of its beauty in the hands of a clumsy translator. The work I read was without exception excellent."

Speechless, Auslander picked angrily at the frayed cuff of her shirt.

"And, naturally, I would expect to pay you whatever fee you are accustomed to receiving. I am hardly a wealthy man—as I say, I am a student. 'Independently poor' is how I might describe my financial status"—that curious little laugh again—"but this of course is important, it is not a luxury."

Auslander could not think of what to say. She looked around at the disorder in her bedroom, a tiny perfect square littered with clothes and papers and precarious towers of books, and through the doorway, into the kitchen, where the tub stood full on its stubby clawed legs. The water was probably cold as a stone by now.

"All right," she said finally. "I'll meet with you. But only for half an hour, no more. Is that understood?" Even as she spoke these cautionary words she felt foolish, ashamed of herself.

But he was not offended. "That's fine," he said. "That's fine." She had been prepared for a crow of triumph. Yet he sounded neither triumphant nor relieved. Instead he had turned distracted; his tone was distant. Auslander had a sudden clear vision of him thinking: All right, now this is settled. On to the other.

They set a time and place, and Auslander—herself relieved that the conversation was over—hung up the phone and went into the kitchen. The bathwater had indeed turned quite cold. As she drained some of it and watched the tap steam out a rush of fresh hot water, she resolved to put the Rumanian out of her mind. The tenor of the conversation had left her feeling vaguely anxious, but there was nothing to be done for it. She would know soon enough what she had gotten herself into. She would undoubtedly be sorry, that much was already clear. It seemed to her that she was always getting herself into something about which she would be certain to be sorry later.

❁

In truth, Auslander at thirty-four had no serious regrets about her life. For all her small miscalculations, all the momentary lapses in judgment that only proved to her that she'd do better to attend to her instincts, in the end there was nothing that upset the steady balance she'd attained. She had lived in the same small Greenwich Village apartment for a dozen years; she had a few friends she trusted and who did not make especially great demands on her time or spirit; her work was work she liked and excelled in. The work in particular was a real source of pleasure to her; and yet it was not the work she had set out to do. She had begun as a poet, and she had not, she thought, been a very bad one. Still, she had known by her freshman year at college that she would never be a very good one. She had been able to tell the difference even then between true poets and those who were only playing at it for their own amusement. Poetry as self-examination or catharsis was not for her—not enough for her—and knowing she would never be one of the few real poets, she gave it up without too much sorrow.

The decision to make her way as a translator of other, better, poets' work was one that hardly needed to be made: she found she had been moving toward it steadily for years, as if by intent. As early as the fifth grade she had discovered that languages came easily to her: the Hebrew lessons her father had insisted on were a snap, a pleasure; Yiddish, which was spoken at home, she taught herself to read and write. In junior high school she learned French, swallowing up long lists

of words as if she'd been hungering for them all her young
life. At that age she took this as a matter of course; it was only
later that she came to understand that facility with languages
was considered a talent, a special gift. By her sixteenth birthday she was fully fluent in French, Hebrew, Yiddish, and Span-
ish. By eighteen she had added German and Italian, and by
the time she had completed her undergraduate education she
had mastered Portuguese, Rumanian, and Russian as well. Her
choice to become a translator, she knew, was a kind of com-
promise between aspirations and ability; but it was a compro-
mise that satisfied her.

She knew her limits. This, Auslander believed, was
her best trait. She did not deceive herself and thus could not
disappoint herself. She always knew where she stood. She
was aware, for example, that she was not a beauty. She was
content with her looks, however, for they were certainly good
enough ("for my purposes," she had told a former lover, a
painter who had wondered aloud if she were ever sad about
not being "a more conventionally pretty type"). When she
troubled to make even a halfhearted effort she was quite attractive—neatly if eccentrically dressed, solid looking, "an in-
domitable gypsy," in the words of the painter. Her unruly black
hair and eyebrows, her wide forehead and prominent nose,
her fine posture—about which her father had been insistent
along with the Hebrew classes—all of this made an impression. Her figure, another ex-lover had told her, was that of a
Russian peasant—he meant her strong legs and broad shoulders and hips. The notion amused her (though the man, finally, did not; he was a biochemist with little in the way of real
imagination, and his stolidness, which she had at first inter-
preted as a charming imperturbability, depressed her after several months). She knew she was the kind of woman of whom
other women said, "She's really very striking don't you think?"
to men who shrugged and agreed, without actually looking at
her, in order to keep the peace. And yet there was a particular

sort of man who appreciated her brand of attractiveness—men by and large a decade or so older than herself, intelligent and good-natured men who had a tendency to brood, even to be sullen, and whose wit was marked by self-criticism. In any case, she was not "on the market." She had no call to compete with the slim, lively blondes or the dramatic dark young beauties who weaved like lovely ribbons through the city, brilliantly pretty and perpetually bored and lonely. Auslander watched them at publication parties and post-reading parties, in Village cafés and restaurants and bars, and she eavesdropped on their talk with mild interest: there was a hunt on in the city; there was always talk—she heard it everywhere—about the lack of available, desirable men. Auslander herself was not lonely, never bored. She liked having a man in her life, and frequently she did, but she was most at ease alone, and she grew uncomfortable when a man tried to force himself too far into her affairs. It made her nervous to have a man poking about in her things, clattering through cabinets and riffling through her books, cooking pasta in her kitchen, sitting casually in her desk chair.

Auslander's boyfriends (a ridiculous word, she thought, when the men she knew were over forty; though, curiously, the men themselves seemed to like it) always started off admiring her "independence" and "self-sufficiency." Later, they would accuse her of "fear of commitment," "obsessive self-reliance." Her most recent affair, with a poet named Farrell—a very good poet, whose work she admired greatly, and the first, and only, poet with whom she had ever been involved in this way—had dissolved after nearly a year into a series of nasty arguments: he called her inflexible and cold; she pronounced him infantile, morbidly dependent. In the end she slept with a young novelist she met at the Ninety-second Street Y, and carelessly let Farrell discover it. He drank himself into a rage and howled at her, pounding the refrigerator and the bathtub with his fists, and hurled a bottle of shampoo across the room; the plastic split and pale orange globs spattered the walls. She watched in mute amazement as he flung himself around her kitchen in a fury, bellowing like an animal. Finally she slammed out of the apartment without a word, and when she returned an hour and a half later he was asleep on her bedroom floor, curled like a shell among her clothes. She spent the night sitting wide awake and shivering at her desk, and in the morning when he rose she sat staring at him until he nodded and said, "Well, all right, then," and left.

She had not seen him since—it had been five weeks now—and she had found that she missed him. This itself was disturbing. If he was gone, she wanted him gone: done with. She yearned for clarity; ambivalence she detested. They had been a bad match, she reminded herself. Farrell was so demanding, and what did he want from her, after all? To be a different sort of person than she was? To take care of him? He needed constant attention. Still, there was no getting around the fact that she liked him. More than liked him. She was able to admit to herself that she was fonder of him than she had been of anyone in years—perhaps ever in her life. She wasn't even entirely sure why she had slept with the young writer except that she had felt suffocated. She'd needed to poke her way out, shake things up. But she had taken a good deal of pleasure in Farrell's company before their battling had begun.

This had happened again and again, this cycle of pleasure and discontent. Auslander could not help but wonder sometimes if she were simply picking the wrong men. To hear other women talk, most men were afraid of involvement. Her friend Delia, a playwright, had confessed to her that the man she'd been seeing for the last two years complained constantly about feeling trapped. "He says he wants to be close," she told Auslander, "but then he admits that the whole notion of togetherness terrifies him." Why then was it that the men Auslander knew seemed only too eager to cast in their lots with her? Delia laughed. She said, "Oh, sure. You ought to try taking one of them up on it sometime. He'd be out the door so fast you wouldn't know what hit you. Take Farrell, for instance. Do you think he'd know what to do with you if he had you? He'd be scared to death."

Auslander was not so sure. Not that it mattered anymore. Farrell, she felt certain, was out of the picture for good. They had spoken on the phone a number of times, but he was still angry with her, and the last time they'd talked—he had telephoned her, drunk, in the dead middle of the night—he had called her a "cold ungiving bitch."

It was of Farrell that Auslander was thinking as she readied herself for her appointment with Petru Viorescu. It wasn't that she was imagining a romance with the Rumanian. She expected that she would read a few of his poems, gently tell him that she could not translate them, and they would never meet again. No, it was only that this was the first time in more than a month that she had dressed and tidied herself knowing that she was going to meet with a man. She had been keeping to herself since the explosion with Farrell, seeing only the occasional woman friend—Delia or Margot or Kathleen, all of whom lived nearby—for lunch or coffee. She had not even attended a reading or seen a play or a movie since that night. It struck her now that it was as if she had been in hiding. Hiding from what? she wondered, surprised at herself. Afraid that Farrell would sneak up behind her on the street or in a theater? And if he did? What did it matter?

Displeased, she shook off the thought and took a few steps back from the full-length mirror behind her bedroom door, considering herself. She grimaced. What a specter! Brushing and tugging and straightening, turning this way and that. There was something demeaning, Auslander thought, about thinking of one's appearance. Still, it could not be avoided. She tipped her head, squinting at herself. She looked all right. She had decided it would be wise to appear a trifle stern, and in gray corduroy slacks and a black sweater, boots, no jewelry, no scarves, her hair in a single long braid, she was satisfied that she had achieved the appropriate effect. Nodding to herself, she swept out of the room, snatched up her long coat and her gloves, and was off, even looking forward to the meeting now as a kind of mild diversion.

In the Peacock Café she had no trouble spotting him. He had the hollow, unhealthy look of a youngish poet—mid-thirties, she guessed, somewhat older than she had expected, and wore the uniform of a graduate student: unpressed shirt and tie, corduroy jacket and blue jeans. He was very slight. As she took him in with a glance from the doorway, she calculated that he was about her own height, or not much taller. He sat smoking a cigarette and tapping a teaspoon against a coffee mug at one of the small round tables in the front of the café.

Auslander went in flourishing her coat and smacking her gloves together, her braid flapping behind her, and moved straight to his table and extended her hand. "Mr. Viorescu?"

He started, and half-stood so abruptly the mug clattered against the sugar bowl. "Ah, Miss Auslander?"

Auslander nodded and sat down across from him. There was an alert, tensely intelligent look about him, she thought—almost an animal-like keenness.

"You are younger than I had imagined," he said. His presence of mind seemed to have returned to him. He was assessing her quite coolly.

She thought of saying: You are older and shorter. But she only nodded.

"I don't know why I should have expected that you would be older—perhaps fifty." He grinned and tilted back his chair, folding his arms across his chest. His smile made her uncomfortable and reminded her that the meeting was not likely to be a pleasant one for her. "Would you like a cappuccino? Or an espresso perhaps?"

"American coffee, thank you." She decided not to remove her coat; she would make it clear that she meant to stick by her half-hour time limit. Viorescu continued to grin at her, and she was relieved when the waitress finally idled by to take her order. They sat in silence until she returned with the coffee. Then the Rumanian leaned forward and placed his hands flat on the table. "I know you are busy, so I shall come to the point immediately. Would you be interested in undertaking the translation of the work of a poet who is, I assure you, quite brilliant, a magnificent talent, and who has never been published in English?"

Auslander raised her eyebrows. "I see you are not of the opinion that modesty is a virtue."

"Modesty?" Momentarily he was confused. Then, at once, he began to laugh. "Oh, yes, that is very good, very good."

Auslander, herself confused, did not know what to say.

"I am so sorry—I should have realized. You of course imagined that I was the poet. Yes, I would have drawn the same conclusion." He chuckled softly. "Ah, but my God, imagine me a poet! A fond wish, as it happens, but without even the smallest glimmer of hope." He shook his head. "No, no, look here. It is my wife of whom I am speaking. The poet Teodora Viorescu."

"You're not a poet?"

"Not in the slightest." He lifted his hands from the table and turned them palms up. "As it happens, I have no ability in this area at all. In fact, I have thought to try to translate a number of my wife's poems. I believed I might manage it. But I find it takes a poet to do such work, or—you said you were not yourself a poet?—a rather exceptional talent which I do not possess. It was a hopeless task, hopeless. The results were. . . earthbound. Do you know what I mean by this? The poetry was lost."

Auslander sipped her coffee as she mulled this over. Finally she said, "Your wife . . . I take it she is unable to translate her own work?"

"Ah, well, you see, this is the problem. She has not the command of English I have. She has had some . . . some reluctance to learn the language as fully as she might. Oh, she is able to express herself perfectly well in spoken English. As for writing . . . that is another matter altogether."

"Yes." Auslander nodded. "This is often the case."

"I had hoped you might recognize her name, though it is understandable if you do not. Her reputation was only beginning to become established in our country when we left. She was thought of then as one of the most promising young poets in Rumania. She was very young, you understand—nineteen—but still she had published a small book and her work was included in two quite prestigious anthologies."

"Viorescu," Auslander murmured. "She has always published under this name?"

"Yes. We married when she was seventeen."

"Seventeen!"

He shrugged. "We have known each other since we were children. I was the best friend of her eldest brother."

"I see," Auslander said politely.

"And in any case, over the last eight years you most certainly would not have heard of her. Since we came to the United States there has been nothing to hear."

"She is not writing?"

"Oh, she is writing, she is writing all the time. But she writes only in Rumanian. None of the work has been published."

"How is it that she has never before had any interest in having her poems translated?"

"Well, it is somewhat more complicated than that." He shifted in his seat. "You see, even now she insists she has no interest."

"But . . ." Auslander narrowed her eyes. "You're discussing this with me without her permission then?"

He poked at his pack of cigarettes with his index finger,

pushing it around in a small circle. His eyes followed its path.

"You must realize that I could not possibly consider the translation of a writer's work against her wishes," Auslander said.

He did not raise his eyes. "Well, here is the problem," he said. "I am very . . . I am concerned about her. She is not—how can I say this correctly? She is not adjusting. She is languishing here. A poet needs a certain amount of attention to thrive. Teo is not thriving. Thus I fear for her."

"Still it doesn't seem—"

"*We* are not thriving," he said. Now he looked at Auslander. "She sits awake late at night and writes; the poems she puts in a drawer in the bedroom. She will not discuss them. She refuses to consider the possibility of their translation. She is angry—all the time she seems angry. Often she will not even speak to me."

"Well, this is a personal matter," Auslander said, "between the two of you only."

He continued as if she had not spoken. "Teo is rather frail, you see. She has headaches, she does not sleep well. Frequently she is depressed. I feel strongly that she cannot continue this way. She has no life outside her part-time job at the university. She has no friends, no one to talk with. She says I am her only friend. And it was I who took her away from her family and a promising career."

"She is sorry she left Rumania?"

"Not quite sorry, no. The situation there was untenable, impossible. Worse for her than for me. She is a Jew—only nominally, of course; it was virtually impossible to practice Judaism in our country—but this in itself made life difficult for her. No, we were completely in agreement about leaving. But here . . .she is always unhappy. Her poetry, her most recent work—it makes me weep to read it, it is so full of sorrow. The poems are spectacular: violent and beautiful. But it is as if she is speaking only to herself."

"Perhaps this is the way she wants it."

Again he ignored her. "I have thought for a long time about finding a translator for her. I believe that if she were able to hold in her hand a translation of one of her poems, if it were precisely the right translation—she would change her mind. But how to find the person capable of this! It was daunting to me; it seemed beyond my abilities. When I read your essay in *Metaphrasis*, however, I was certain I had found Teo's translator. I have no doubt of this, still. I feel it, I feel it in my heart. As I read that essay, it was like a sign: I knew you were the one. With absolute clarity I knew also that you would be sympathetic to the problem . . . the unusual situation."

"Naturally, I'm sympathetic. But what can I do? Without her approval I could not translate a word of her writing. Surely you understand that. What you're asking of me is not only unethical, it's unfeasible. Without the participation of your wife . . ." She shook her head. "I'm sorry. It's impossible."

Viorescu's expression was impassive as he tapped a cigarette from his pack and placed it between his lips. As he lit it, he breathed out, in rapid succession, two dark streams of smoke.

"But I would still like to see some of her poems," Auslander said. She did not know herself if she were being merely polite or if he had indeed called upon her curiosity. In any case it seemed to her necessary to make this offer; she could not refuse to read his wife's work after all he had said.

Viorescu took the cigarette from his mouth and looked at it. Then he waved it at Auslander. "Ah, yes, but are you quite sure that this itself would not be 'unethical'?"

His petulance, she decided, was excusable under the circumstances. He was disappointed; this was understandable. Calmly, she said, "I see no reason why it should be." She kept her eyes on his cigarette as she spoke. "Unless, of course, you would simply prefer that I not read them."

He smiled, though faintly. "No, no. I had hoped that in any event you would want to read them." From a satchel hung on the back of his chair he produced a manila envelope. He laid it on the table between them. It was quite thick. The sight of it moved her, and this came as a surprise. Viorescu folded his hands and set them atop the envelope. "I have chosen mostly those poems written in the last year or so, but also there is a quantity of her earlier work, some of it dating from our first few years in this country. I have also included a copy of her book, which I thought you would be interested in seeing."

"Yes," Auslander said. "I would, thank you."

"It is, I believe, a fair sample of Teo's work. It should give you a true sense of what she is about. See for yourself that I have not been overly generous in my praise."

"You're very proud of her."

"Yes, naturally." He spoke brusquely enough so that Auslander wondered if she had offended him. "Perhaps this is hard for you to understand. Teo is . . . she is not only my wife, she is like my sister. I have known her since she was six years old and I was twelve. We were family to each other long before our marriage."

A dim alarm went off in Auslander's mind—a warning that confidences were ahead. This was her cue to change the subject, no question about it. But she remained silent. Altogether despite herself she was touched.

"Ah, you find this poignant," Viorescu said, startling her.

Embarrassed, she nodded.

"Yes, well, perhaps it is. That we have been so close for so much of our lives is itself touching, I suppose. But we are not . . . . She is . . . . Ah, well." He shrugged and smiled, vaguely.

Auslander cautioned herself: This is none of your business; you want no part of this. But she felt drawn in; she could not help asking, "What were you about to say?" And yet as she spoke she groaned inwardly.

"Oh—only that something has been lost. This is maybe not so unusual after so many years, I think." He closed his eyes for an instant. "Something lost," he murmured. "Yes, it may be that she is lost to me already. Well, it is my own fault. I have not been a help to her. I have done a great deal of damage."

At once Auslander realized she did not want to hear any of this. Not another word, she thought, and she imagined herself rising, bidding him goodbye and taking off—she did not even have to take the package of poems. What was the point of it? Did she honestly think there was a chance she might discover a hidden genius? Who was she kidding?

"It is very bad, very bad," he muttered.

A mistake, Auslander thought. Sitting here listening, offering to read the poetry of his wife—all a mistake. She could feel her chest tightening against what was certain to be a perilous intrusion into her life. For it would get worse with every moment: confessions led to further confessions. *No more.* She wanted no more of Viorescu and his poet wife.

He pushed the envelope toward her. "Here, I can see you are impatient. I did not mean to keep you so long."

She picked up the envelope. "It's true, I should be going." She half-rose, awkwardly, and drew the envelope to her chest. "Ah—shall I phone you after I've read these?"

"I will phone you." He smiled at her, broadly this time. "I should like to thank you in advance for your time. I am very grateful."

Auslander felt uneasy. "I hope I've made it completely clear that I'm not going to be able to take Teodora on."

"After you have read the poems," he said, "perhaps you will change your mind."

"I'm afraid not."

"You have agreed to read them, after all."

"I am always interested in good poetry," Auslander said stiffly. "If your wife's work is as you say, I would be doing myself a disservice by not reading it."

"Indeed," he said, and now he laughed—his telephone laugh, that short curious bark. "I will phone you next week."

She could feel his eyes on her back as she retreated, the envelope of poems under her arm. For his sake—and for the sake of the unknown, unhappy Teodora—she hoped the poems were not dreadful. She did not have much confidence in this hope, however; the excitement that had begun to stir in her only moments ago had already left her entirely.

By the time she had passed through the café's door and emerged onto the street, she was convinced the work would turn out to be inept. As she crossed Greenwich Avenue, her coat whipping about her legs, her head bowed against the wind, she was imagining her next conversation with Viorescu. She would be gentle; there would be no need to tell him the truth about his wife's work. If he deceived himself, he deceived himself. It was not her responsibility.

❂

As it turned out, Viorescu had neither lied to her nor deceived himself. Teodora Viorescu's poems were extraordinary. Auslander, after reading the first of them, which she had idly extracted from the envelope and glanced at as she sat down to her dinner, had in her astonishment risen from the table, dropping her fork to her plate, and reached for the envelope to shake out the remainder of its contents. A batch of poems in hand, she ate her broiled chicken and rice without the slightest awareness of so doing. She could hardly believe her eyes. The poems jumped on the pages, full of terror, queer dangerous images of tiny pointed animal faces, blood raining through the knotted black branches of trees, fierce woods which concealed small ferocious creatures. And the language! The language was luminous, electrifying. What a haunted creature

the poet herself must be! Auslander thought as she at last col-
lapsed against her pillows at half-past twelve. She had been
reading for five hours, had moved from table to desk to bed,
and she had not yet read all the poems Viorescu had given
her; but she intended to, tonight. She needed, however, to rest
for a moment. She was exhausted; her eyes burned.

For ten minutes she lay listening to the dim apartment-
sounds of night: refrigerator, plumbing, upstairs creaks and
groans, downstairs murmurs. Then she sat up again, stacked
her pillows neatly behind her, and set again to reading. When
she had read all of the poems once she began to reread; after a
while she got up and fetched a legal pad. For some time she
reread and made notes on the pad, resisting with difficulty the
urge to go to her desk for a batch of the five-by-seven cards
she used to make notes on work she was translating. Finally
she gave in, telling herself it was simply easier to use the index
cards, their feel was more familiar, and with a supply of the
cards beside her she worked until dawn in something of a fe-
verish state, feeling like one of the poet's own strange night
creatures as she sat wild-haired and naked in her bed, chewing on her fingers and the end of her pen, furiously scratching
out notes as the gray-bluish light rose around her.

For days, anxiously, she awaited Viorescu's call. On
the fifth day she checked the telephone directory and was half-
relieved to find no listing; she knew she should not phone him.
But she felt foolish, waiting. She was reminded of her adoles-
cence—hateful time—as she stared at the phone, willing it to
ring. After each of her ventures out of the apartment—her
few forays to the supermarket and the library and the
laundromat, her one trip uptown to return the galleys of a historical romance—she hastened to her answering machine. The
playbacks yielded up several invitations to functions that didn't
interest her, calls from friends, two calls from her mother, one
from Farrell.

"Do you miss me, Harriet my love? Are you lonely?"

Auslander breathed impatiently, fists against her thighs. Farrell's message was intended of course to make her angry. He never called her "Harriet" except to taunt her. Well, let him, she thought. She would not allow it, she would not allow *him*, to upset her. She had been less preoccupied lately with missing him; she had other things on her mind (and she'd like the chance to tell him that, she thought)—though the sound of his voice on the tape, it was true, sent a shiver of sorrow and loneliness through her. "Has it hit you yet that you're all alone? And are you enjoying it, as anticipated? Or are you sorry? Or are you not alone—have you already found someone else to resist loving?" There was a pause, then, harsher: "Don't call me back. I've changed my mind; I don't want to talk to you after all."

Eight days passed; then nine. On the tenth day—once again as she was about to take a bath, one leg over the side of the tub—the phone rang and she knew instantly it was the poet's husband.

He was cheerful. "So? What do you make of my Teo?"

Auslander felt it would be wise to be guarded. "Well, she's something, all right. An original, no question."

"You enjoyed her work, then?"

She could not remain cautious; she was too relieved to hear from him. "'Enjoyed?' Ha! She's a terror, your wife. The real thing, astonishing stuff."

Viorescu was cackling. "Yes, yes, it's true, absolutely true. She is one of a kind, a wonder, a gem!"

Auslander stood beside the bed coiling and uncoiling the telephone cord about her wrist as they went on to talk about the poems. She excused herself to get her notes, and then she was able to quote directly from them; Viorescu was delighted. She had just launched into some observations about one of the most recent poems when she happened to glance up and saw that the man across the way was standing at his window staring blankly at her. Good lord, she thought, he would begin to imagine she strolled around naked for his benefit. She sat down on the bed, her back to the window, and pulled the blanket up around her.

"Listen, Petru," she said, "I've been thinking. I really ought to meet Teodora."

He clicked his tongue. "Well, as you know, this is not such a simple matter. I am not sure it is possible at all right now."

"It may be difficult," she said, "but surely we can manage it. If we two put our heads together—"

"Tell me, have you given any further thought to the question of translating her work?"

"I've already told you I would not consider it without her full cooperation."

"But you are interested! Well, this is good news indeed. Of course you must meet her. Let me think . . . . Why don't you come to dinner? Let us say, next Friday night?"

"But are you sure?"

"Yes, of course. Though it would be best not to let her know from the start that you are a translator."

Auslander was discomfited. "Are you sure that's necessary? If I'm not to be a translator, who am I? How did we meet?"

"Oh, I shall say I met you at an academic function. Teo never attends department functions with me."

"An academic function," Auslander echoed. She recalled then that she had never asked him what his area of study was. "What department is it that I am to be associated with?"

"Philosophy," he said with a short laugh. "That is my department. My specialization is Nietzsche."

"Wonderful," Auslander said. "You can tell Teo I'm a renowned Nietzsche scholar and I'll remain silent all evening."

"I can tell her that you are Hannah Arendt and she would not know the difference," Viorescu said dryly.

"Are you sure all this intrigue is necessary? Maybe you ought to simply tell her the truth."

"No. She would suspect a plot."

"Has she such a suspicious nature?"

"It does not take much," he said, "to arouse suspicious thoughts. Why take such a chance? We can tell her the truth after an hour, two hours perhaps, once she is comfortable in your presence."

For the second time, Auslander hung up the phone after talking to the Rumanian and found herself wondering what she was letting herself in for. Gloomily she paced around her bedroom—the man across the way, she noted as she went to the window to pull down the shade, was no longer looking out—and tried to convince herself that she was in no danger of becoming personally involved with the Viorescus. They needed a translator, she told herself; it was not necessary to be their friend. Still, she didn't like the circumstances; they did not lend themselves to a smooth working relationship. Even assuming that all went well—that Teodora was willing, that she could be reasoned with—the project was likely to be full of difficulties and strains, starting out the way it was. Already she had agreed to this preposterous masquerade! It was clear enough that between Viorescu and his wife there were problems, serious problems. Auslander hated the thought of these complications.

But the poetry! Auslander shook her head, tugged at her hair as she circled the room. *Oh, the poetry!*

❂

She would have recognized Teodora Viorescu at once, Auslander felt. Had she passed her on Sixth Avenue a day or two ago, she was certain she would have thought: Might this not be the poet? Small and pale, with hair like a slick black cap cut so short her ears stuck out pointedly from beneath it, she felt her way through the room toward Auslander like a swimmer.

"I'm very pleased to meet you," Auslander said. "Petru has told me a great deal about you." She took the poet's small hand in hers. It was very cold.

"So you are Miss Auslander."

"Just Auslander is fine."

"Ah, yes, so my husband told me." She smiled. Her face was perfectly round, her eyes also—oddly—round. How white her skin was! As if she truly never saw daylight. And how grave she looked, even as she smiled. It was in the eyes, Auslander thought. Her eyes were the eyes of one of her own imaginary creatures: liquid-black with floating pinpoints of light, emitting a steady watchful beam.

During dinner there was small talk. The food was Rumanian, traditional, Viorescu explained. He seemed very nervous and spoke at length about ingredients and methods of cooking. Auslander avoided meeting his eyes; she was sure it was plain to Teodora that something was up. Teodora herself kept her eyes downcast and picked at her food; between the Viorescus barely a word passed.

Auslander helped Viorescu move the table back into the kitchen and pile the dishes in the sink; he tried to whisper to her but she waved him away impatiently. Enough of this, she thought. She returned to the living room to find the poet sitting on the windowseat, gazing out upon Riverside Drive. Auslander seated herself on the end of the couch nearest the window and said, "Please, Teodora, won't you tell me about your work? Your husband informs me that you are a fine poet."

"There is nothing to tell." She turned slowly toward Auslander. Her tone and facial expression were remote. Auslander recalled what Farrell had told her when she'd described a famous poet she'd met as "terribly cool and remote." "Wrong again, Auslander," he had said. "Not *remote*. Only massively depressed and riddled with anxiety— like me."

Auslander tried again. "Petru tells me you published a book in Rumania."

"Yes."

"And have you any interest in publishing your work in the United States?"

Teodora glanced over at her husband, who had entered the room silently and positioned himself by the bookshelves opposite the couch where Auslander sat, and spoke quietly to him in Rumanian. Auslander heard only snatches of what she said. "Unfair"—she heard this word several times—and "You should have told me." Once, clearly, she heard the poet say "unforgivable," and then—her heart sank—she heard unmistakably the Rumanian for "translator." Viorescu did not speak. Finally Teodora turned again to Auslander. "I am sorry if we have put you to any trouble. I do not wish for my work to be translated into English." Abruptly she stood and left the room.

Auslander started to rise, but Viorescu said, "Please, Auslander. There is nothing we can do."

"What do you mean 'nothing we can do'?" Auslander was astounded. "I thought you were so eager to convince her."

"I believed she might be convinced. Apparently I was wrong."

"But you didn't even *try*."

"It would be pointless. She is very angry at having been deceived."

"Why didn't you just tell her what I was here for in the first place?"

"You must realize that it would not have mattered either way. She is obviously beyond—"

"You're giving up. I can't believe it. You do this whole . . ." She sank back into the couch and looked up at him in amazement. "And giving up so easily!"'

"Easily!" He laughed hoarsely. "I have been trying for years to talk her into having her work translated. I am giving up now *finally*." He shook his head. "There is a story—do you know it?—about a famous philosopher who decided, after long consideration, to become a vegetarian. For many years he lived as a vegetarian. He spoke and wrote of it, of course, since under the circumstances such a decision could not be a private matter only. He spoke brilliantly, in fact, and movingly on the moral logic of his choice. Then one day he sat down to his table and began to eat a steak. His students, as you would suppose, were quite agitated when they saw this. Why the change? they cried. What had happened? And the famous philosopher said, 'Ah, well, it was time to give it a rest.'"

"There is no relevance to this story, Petru," Auslander said wearily.

"Oh, I quite disagree, Auslander, my friend. But in any event don't you find it a charming story?"

"I have other things on my mind," she said. "Tell me. Why *doesn't* Teo want her work translated? What does she say when you ask her?"

"She says, 'Because I say so.'"

"But that's a child's logic."

"No. It's a parent's logic, rather. The child asks, 'Why not?' The parent says, 'Only because I say not.'"

"Well, then." Auslander shrugged and stood up. She was angrier and more disappointed than she could have predicted. "I guess that's it. Shall I mail the poems back to you?"

"Are you in a rush to be rid of them?" He smiled at her. "No, my friend. Let us not altogether give up. May I telephone you tomorrow?"

"What's the point?"

"Oh, I shall talk to her tonight. Perhaps it would be wise to tell her you've already read her work, extend your compliments. It will depend on her spirits."

"But I thought..." Auslander stopped herself. There was no sense trying to follow him. "All right, fine. Call me."

"Tell me something," he said as he walked with her to the door and helped her into her coat. "Are you absolutely certain that if her work were translated it would be publishable here?"

"Oh, without question," Auslander said. Then a thought came to her. "Why? Do you think it will help if Teo knows this? Because if you like, I can make a few calls tomorrow, I can ask around, get a feel for it." Instantly she regretted this offer. Who on earth could she call to discuss the work of an untranslated Rumanian poet? Without the poems to show, what could she expect an editor to say? It was absurd.

"That would be very kind."

"I should go now," Auslander said, her hand on the doorknob. As she went down the hall to the elevator, she reflected that it was a miracle that she had escaped without having made any further promises.

On the IRT heading back to the Village, she removed from her Danish schoolbag the envelope containing Teodora's poems. She was not sure why she hadn't told Viorescu she had the poems with her—evidently, she thought, she wasn't ready yet to part with them. She flipped through the pages until she found the one she wanted. From the front pocket of her bag she took out a pen and the packet of index cards she had begun to keep on Teodora's work, and she sifted through the cards, stopping at the one headed "In the Cold Field, In the Troubled Light." She ran her eyes quickly down the card; besides the title, she had already, automatically, cast a number of lines into English as she made her notes. She sighed and turned to the poem itself. Then, pen in hand, using the canvas bag as a lap-desk, she began the translation.

❁

❂

He did not even bother to say hello. "She wants no part of it," Viorescu announced. "She will not discuss it."

"What did you tell her? Did you explain—"

"I pleaded, I made promises, I was a madman." He laughed miserably. "She made me sleep on the couch."

"That's none of my affair," Auslander said sharply.

"I want to apologize for all the trouble you have taken."

"Yes, well, here's a surprise for you," she said. She took a deep breath and then she told him about the poems she had translated last night, working until four o'clock, until she couldn't see clearly anymore.

"My God, that's. . . Is this really true? How marvelous! Please, will you read them to me?"

For half an hour she read Viorescu his wife's poems. She had rough versions—very rough in some cases—of eight poems already; one or two poems were quite polished, almost perfect, Auslander thought.

"But this is wonderful! Incredible! Oh, we *must* convince her. Do you think . . .what if we did as I had planned to begin with . . ."

"Petru," Auslander said. "*Think*. If you were to show her these translations she might get very angry. She might— quite justifiably—feel invaded."

"She might feel complimented."

"She might. You would know better than I."

Auslander was not altogether sure of this, however. His track record did not seem to be the best.

Several days passed. Auslander continued to translate the poems. There was no logic in it, she knew; she had almost no hope by now that Teodora would agree to have this done. She was translating the poems because she wanted to; there was no other reason. She was working at it late on Saturday afternoon when there was a knock on her door. Surprised, her first thought was of Farrell. No one ever dropped by without calling. Farrell himself had done so only once, and she had explained then how much she disliked unannounced visits; he would surely do it now only if he were drunk. Cautiously she went to the door and stood listening.

"Auslander, are you there?"

It was Petru Viorescu. She snapped away the police lock and swung the door open. He looked terrible.

"Petru! What on earth's the matter?"

"May I come in?" He brushed past her and heaved himself into her desk chair. He looked around. "What is this room? Bathroom, study, kitchen?"

Auslander closed and locked the door. "What's going on? You look like hell."

"I want to tell you something. I need to discuss this with someone. I am going to lose my mind."

"Is it about Teodora?" she asked anxiously. "Has something happened?"

"Oh, something has happened, yes, but not what you imagine. You think she is so fragile! You are afraid that she has perhaps tried to commit suicide, that she has had a 'nervous breakdown.' No," he said. "She is made of iron, my wife." He laughed, but after a second he placed his head in his hands and began to weep. Auslander stood back, uncertain what was expected of her. Finally he stopped crying; he looked up at her and very calmly told his story. He had met a young woman, someone in his department. He was in love; there was nothing to be done for it.

"I don't understand," Auslander said. "When did this happen? Just this week?"

"Months ago," he said. "Months."

"But I don't understand," she said. "Have you . . .?"

"I have not slept with her, if that is your question."

"But then . . . I still don't understand. Have you told Teo about this?"

"Of course." He seemed offended at the implication

that he might not have.

"But why? You haven't done anything, Petru. What is there to tell? You have a crush, is that right? Is that—"

"No, no. It is not a crush. I am in love."

Auslander was at a loss. "Well, what do you want to do?" Then immediately she said, "Never mind. I don't want to know."

He began to weep again. Auslander wanted to scream. Suddenly a suspicion came to her. "Tell me something," she said. "How much does this business with the other woman—"

"Ana," Viorescu said.

"I don't want to know her name! How much does it have to do with Teo's refusal to have the poems translated?"

"How much does anything have to do with anything?"

"Don't speak to me that way, I won't stand for it," she snapped at him. "Answer me truthfully." She began to pace around the kitchen. "What's going on here? What is this all about? When did you tell Teo about this woman?"

"Months ago," he said. "As soon as I knew. I could not keep my feelings secret from her. We tell each other everything, we always have; we are brother and sister, inseparable."

"But you fancy yourself in love with someone else," she said sarcastically.

"One has nothing to do with the other. You must yourself know that."

"You're not planning to leave Teo?"

"No, I am not going to leave her. The question is whether she will leave me."

"But why has it come to this now, if she's known all these months? What's changed?" At once Auslander had the answer. "Petru," she said, "did the idea of having her poems translated backfire on you in some way?"

He shrugged.

"Did you come up with the notion of getting me to do

this in the first place as a way of . . . placating her? Giving her something of her own? Did you think that having me translate her poems might make things all right between the two of you?"

"This is partly true, yes."

"You could have just bought her flowers," Auslander said bitterly. "It would have saved a lot of trouble."

"I have bought her flowers," he said. "And in any case the trouble, it seems to me, was worth it. No? You don't agree? You understand that this was not the only reason I wanted to have the work translated, do you not? I have been discussing the matter with her for years, years. Long before I knew Ana, long before I met you. Years!" he said angrily. "She will not listen to reason. And what is a poet without readers? I have been her only reader for too long."

Auslander continued to stalk the kitchen, twisting her hands together as she paced. For a long time she did not speak. Finally she sighed and said, "Well, now there are two of us."

"Yes," Viorescu said. "Yes, exactly. Now there are two of us."

○

The call from Teodora the following night woke her.

"I am sorry to be disturbing you at so late an hour," the poet said. "But I will not be long. I wanted only to say one thing. I understand that Petru has been troubling you with problems of a personal nature."

Auslander was too startled to respond.

"I apologize for this," Teodora said. "I want you to know that I have asked him not to trouble you any further."

"Oh, really, it hasn't been all that much trouble," Auslander said.

"In all events he will not be calling you again."

"Oh, that isn't—" Auslander began. But it was too late; she had already hung up.

○

❂

Auslander did not for a moment seriously consider the possibility that she would not hear from Viorescu. Thus she was not in the least surprised when three days later he called. There was a note of hysteria in his voice, however, which alarmed her.

"What is it, Petru? What's wrong now?"

"She wants to leave me! She says she has had enough, she is fed up. Auslander, please, I need your help. Will you call her? Explain to her? Please?"

"Explain what?" Auslander said. "I don't understand it myself."

"Please. She is at home now. I am in the library. You could call her right now and she could talk to you freely, she is alone."

"I'm sorry, I can't."

"But she wants to leave me!"

"Petru, I can't help you with this. It should be plain by now that I can't. There's nothing I can do."

"Yes, there is. But you refuse! You refuse to help!"

Auslander could not think of what else to do, so she hung up the phone. She stood staring at it. It began to ring again instantly.

She lifted the receiver. "Please don't do this," she said.

"Jesus, Auslander, you're right on top of it tonight, aren't you. I haven't even started doing anything yet."

"Oh, Farrell. I thought you were someone else."

"I wish I were."

"Please," she said, "not tonight. Look, I don't mean to be rude, but are you calling to give me the business? Because if you are, I don't think I'm up to it."

"No, actually I thought I'd take my business elsewhere." He was silent for a moment; then he sighed. "You're not laughing, love. What's the matter? Is something really wrong?"

"No, Farrell," she said flatly, "nothing's really wrong."

"Well, shall I tell you why I called? I've got an idea. What if I gave up drinking? How would that be?"

"How would it be how?"

"Come on, Auslander. You've always complained about my drinking. What if I stopped?"

"I don't know." Suddenly she felt like crying.

"Hey, what's going on? Are you really all right? You sound awful."

"I'm all right," she said. Then, after a second, "No, I'm not. I guess I'm not. I don't know."

"Is there anything I can do?"

She shook her head before she remembered that he couldn't see her. "No," she said. "Not a thing."

"Well, what do you think? Do you think it would make a difference? In our relationship, I mean. Do you think it would help?"

"Look, Farrell," she said, "if you want to quit drinking, then quit drinking. You know perfectly well that I think you ought to. I've said it enough times. But if you're going to do it, do it for yourself, not for me. I don't want to be responsible for the decision."

"Oh, sure, that's right. How could I have forgotten? You don't want to be responsible for anything or anyone, do you?"

"Farrell, please."

"Please what? I am making a perfectly reasonable gesture toward straightening things out between us, and you're just tossing it right back in my face."

"That's not what I mean to do."

"No? What do you mean to do, then? Tell me."

"I don't know."

"You don't, do you."

"No." She realized she was gripping the phone so hard her fingers ached. "I don't."

"Tell me something, will you? *Do* you miss me? Ever? Do you even think about me?"

"Of course I think about you. I think about you a lot. I wonder about how your work is going. I wonder how life's treating you."

He laughed softly. "Oh, Auslander, you should know. Life's not treating me at all—I'm paying my own way."

❂

Into bed with her that night she took the envelope of Teodora's poems and all of Farrell's poetry that she had in the apartment—all the poems of his that she had in typescript, all the magazines that had his poems in them, his four chapbooks, even some stray handwritten lines on pages torn from legal pads, which he'd left scattered about the apartment on nights he couldn't sleep. She read all of it, every line, Teodora's and Farrell's both, read until she felt stunned and overburdened, and fell into a sleep that was a kind of stupor. Under the blanket of poems, dreaming, she turned and tossed in her sleep; poems crackled and fluttered, flew off the bed, alighted on the floor.

It was months before she heard from Viorescu again. He called to tell her that Teodora had killed herself. He had returned from the library late at night and found her. There was no note. "She left nothing," he said. He spoke of the funeral and of Teodora's family. Several times he wept, but very quietly. Auslander listened without saying anything. When he had said all he had to say; she waited, expecting to hear herself tell him that she was sorry, but she remained silent. For a moment they were both silent. Finally Viorescu said, "There is something else I must tell you. Teodora destroyed all of her work—all the poems she wrote from the time we left Rumania. I have searched the apartment; she was very thorough. Every copy of every poem is gone."

Now Auslander was able to make herself speak. "I'm very sorry," she said.

"You are not surprised, I imagine."

"That she destroyed her poems? No, I suppose I'm not."

He hesitated. "You understand that you now have the only copy of her work."

"Yes."

Again they were silent.

"You want the poems translated," Auslander said.

"This is not the time to discuss this, of course," he said. "But after a reasonable amount of time has passed, yes."

"Yes, I see," she said.

"And in the meantime you will be careful, will you not?"

"With the poems? Of course."

"Well, then. . . . We will speak."

"Yes."

As she went to her desk and removed the envelope from the center drawer, where it had remained undisturbed for months, Auslander thought briefly of Farrell's poems, which that same morning months ago she had set on the top shelf of her bedroom closet. She saw them in her mind—the bundle of poems secured by a rubber band, surrounded by the accumulated clutter of years: stacks of letters; shoeboxes full of photographs, postcards, canceled checks; spiral-bound notebooks dating back to graduate school. Then the image vanished and she sat down at her desk; she flipped open the oak box in which her index cards were filed and removed the cards on Teodora—the notes and the dozen translations she had done. One at a time she laid the cards on her desk, as slowly and precisely as a storefront fortune teller, spreading them out carefully in a fan, one corner of each card touching the next. When she had come to the end of the cards, she shook the poems themselves out of the envelope. Now the desktop was littered with poetry. For a time she sat looking at all that she had spilled out there. Then she scooped up everything and stood, hugging the papers and cards tightly to her chest. She crossed the kitchen and with some difficulty unhooked the police lock. In the hallway she hesitated for an instant only. Then she moved quickly. With one arm she held the poet's work; with her free hand she pulled open the door to the incinerator chute. It was a matter of seconds; then it was done.

A NEW AND GLORIOUS LIFE

*"and it was clear to both of them that they had still
a long, long road before them ...."*

Chekhov
"The Lady with the Pet Dog"

It was said that a new person was to arrive today. Thus,
Gad remarked dryly to himself—for there was no one else to
whom *to* remark; he sat alone, as he did every morning—the
buzz and murmur, the trill of speculation. He closed his eyes
as he sat spooning oatmeal from his bowl, and let himself imagine a cloud forming, swollen with expectancy, above all of their
heads and rising toward the ceiling of the dining room. A cloud
that would burst, raining disappointment, as soon as the newcomer was actually among them.

Gad (but no one called him that here; he was called
Gad by his friends, of which there were none within two hundred miles) was certain of this. After two weeks he had divined the way things worked. Already he felt sorry for the
person who would join them next. After all, it had taken hardly
twenty-four hours for the others not only to lose whatever interest in *him* they had had before he had arrived but to begin
to actively dislike him. Indeed, it seemed to him that beneath

the surface of camaraderie, the Ping-Pong and pool and poker playing, nightly readings, slide shows, open studios, screenings of incompletely edited and barely comprehensible films, group discussions over wine and Cheetos of "the artistic process," trips to town (eight giggling artists piled into one car, painters and poets in the backseat on the sculptors' laps) and half-drunken midnight walks "to see the moon" or to make offerings (an orange or a roll swiped from the breakfast basket or a copy of a newly finished poem or in a pinch whatever happened to be picked up on the ground along the way: twigs, pebbles, pine cones, leaves) at the graves of the Colony's "beloved founders"—this last a pilgrimage he had declined to make, his first night: one of a short, fatal series, he now understood, of artists' colony *faux-pas*—there was frank, outright hostility to anyone who was less than a perfect fit. If this latest newcomer was not exactly to their liking, he or she would be excluded utterly, almost at once. As he had been.

Demetrius Gadol—Greek Jew by extraction, composer by vocation, described only recently in the *Times'* Arts and Leisure section (*listed*, his wife always made sure to point out when he spoke of the *Times* piece in her earshot; the *description*, she would say—Janet was a great advocate of humility, as well as an expert in his humiliation—was just two sentences long) as one of "Thirty-three Composers Under Forty To Be Reckoned With"—ate his breakfast, listening as all around him the newcomer was discussed. With his eyes closed, it was easy to pick out the threads of gossip amidst all the other morning chitchat, laughter, the rehashing of last night's drunken revelry, the clattering of cutlery to china, the ringing phone outside the dining room and the scrape of a chair ("I'll get it"— "No, please, let me, I'm expecting a call"), the glassy clank of cups replaced thoughtlessly, uncentered, into saucers, the periodic maraca of dry cereal shaken from its box, toast popping at asymmetric, unexpected intervals. The new person, he heard, was a woman. That she'd been assigned one of the choicest bedrooms—so it was reported—in the mansion itself rather than one of the newer "dorms," fitted with twin beds and pressboard bureaus, stirred up a flurry of conjecture. Just how well-known *was* she?

But which studio? somebody asked. No one knew for sure, and a digression followed, about which studios were winterized and how many were occupied. Gad waited for the flow of information to resume. He was surprised by how attentively he waited. Surprised, first; and then ashamed; and finally, decisively, amused. He had always been willing to laugh at himself—it was one of his saving graces, Janet had said long ago (and as this had been one of the very few kind things she had ever said to him about himself, he had chosen to believe it and to keep believing it, even though she had never, in the eighteen years since then, repeated it). Had he not made a little speech—a shocked, stern, self-righteous speech—on his second night in residence in response to the exchange of speculations that had gone on all through dinner that night about the three artists who were due to turn up the next day?

The "let us not forget what we're all here for" speech, he'd heard it called since then. They'd hated him for it. Now he pretended not to listen as somebody mentioned a composing studio, a stone cabin at the far end of the woods. His heart leapt. Since the day of his arrival, he had been the lone composer, as writers of all stripes, painters, sculptors, a printmaker, three "conceptual" artists (including one who called himself a "light"—as in electricity—artist), two filmmakers, a video artist, and an architect came and went. *But she isn't a composer, is she?* someone else said. *No, I think a writer. But where else can they put her?*

Novelist? somebody said. *No, short stories, I think.* And another voice: *Just one collection? Two?* But then someone else—one of the painters, Gad thought—said, *I heard she was a playwright. I thought I heard she might've even won an Obie.*

She must have won something, someone said—followed by laughter, and a series of remarks, again, about the well-appointed bedroom, the one that had been the house's mistress's, in the days before the mansion and its grounds had been turned into a "refuge for the gifted" (as decreed by the master and mistress's Last Will and Testament, portions of which were engraved on small bronze plaques embedded into the stone wall that enclosed the Colony).

Somebody said, *Maybe she's just well-connected.*

Or else pregnant. I've heard they give special attention to pregnant artists.

So that's *how I could get a bigger studio next time.* Laughter, again. The speaker was a man. One of the great hulking sculptors who worked with heavy, manly materials—concrete, steel, lead—and produced unbearably ugly structures to which they gave cryptic titles. Gad shook his head. He sometimes thought, despite the evidence—the one-man shows in SoHo and the published books and grants and prizes—that he was among a bunch of idiots.

That no one seemed to be sure just what the newcomer "did," thought Gad, was a hopeful sign. It meant that no one knew her, which would make it that much harder for her to be swept into the circle that excluded him. If he went out of his way to meet her first (if, say, he happened to be sitting in the armchair just inside the front entrance to the commons room tonight, so that he would be the first to see her when she came in before dinner), perhaps he might make an impression on her that would not be undermined by what the others would say to her later—for it seemed to him that those who had been in attendance when he'd first arrived had passed on their animosity toward him like a contagion to everyone who'd joined them in the fortnight since.

For a moment, as bits of information, rumors and wild guesses were chewed over, spat out, altered, barked about, Gad indulged himself, imagining her. Because it was a pure fact of his life that he found it much easier to get along with smart, young, pretty women than with men—or with women who were neither young nor pleasant to look at (as Janet never tired of pointing out)—he allowed her beauty, youth, and brilliance. Since the day he'd landed here, there had been mostly men, along with a few—it had to be said—homely women. At this, he blushed and ducked his head, as if the women scattered here and there about the dining room might have had the ability to read his mind. But everyone was busy now considering what prize it was the new arrival—Hannah Something, he caught; he had just missed the last name—might have won. *The National Book Award*, someone suggested. *No—some big grant, not a book prize. Not an Obie either. I really don't think she's a playwright.*

No, I think she might be. Maybe that Louisville thing, you know—

Or an NEA.

No, bigger.

The Lottery, somebody said. More laughter. The phone began to ring again. Cereal rasped into a bowl. Toast popped. A spoon swirled, clanked gently, in a cup. *Christ, not a MacArthur*, someone said. Briefly everyone was silent. *A Pulitzer?* Gad heard one of the painters ask, tentatively, breaking the spell. No, no—all the writers were sure that wasn't it.

Long hair, Gad decided. Very long. Dark?

He snapped back to attention when he heard someone ask, *Does anyone know where she's from?*

New York, I think I heard. Chelsea? The Village?

Doesn't she teach? Didn't I hear somewhere that she's at some huge college in the middle of nowhere?

This was of particular interest to him—a New Yorker by, he always said, "both birth and temperament," but a long-time inhabitant himself of the middle of nowhere by virtue of Janet's excellent and irreplaceable job teaching at a Big Ten college. He contemplated the possibility that the (prize-winning? pregnant?) writer taught at the same school as Janet. If she were a playwright, she'd be in the theater department, and it was not only possible but likely that she and Janet would not ever have crossed paths—there was so vast a bureaucratic gulf between the School of the Arts and the School of Humanities, in which Janet taught. And although he taught too, upon occasion (an undergraduate course for non-music majors, a bone thrown to him once every year or two thanks to the University's "significant other advocacy" policy, which generously—so he always said—included husbands), and "his" department was *in* the School of the Arts, as a lecturer he was practically invisible, was invited to nothing, and met no one except his own current students; he didn't even know where the theater department *was*.

Of course, if she wrote fiction—there seemed still to be debate about this—and it turned out that she taught at Janet's school, it was even possible (here was a sobering thought) that they were *friends*. Janet, long ago, had wanted to write—had written, in fact, as he recalled, in college, when they had first met: bad short stories and poems, which she had required him to praise—before she (as Janet herself put it) "found herself" in graduate school. She still liked to hang around with writers. Her book, which had also been her dissertation—*Trials and Metamorphoses: On the Work of Franz Kafka and Philip Roth*—gave her the credentials, she thought, not only for tenure in her own department, Comparative Studies, but for what she insisted on calling "the literary life."

Gad sighed. Around him, they were winding down. Breakfast dishes were being taken to the kitchen; final cups of coffee were being gulped; fruit from the bowl and tea bags were stuffed into pockets. The conversation was dwindling. There seemed to be no more information; they were down to wondering if it should be considered complimentary or insulting for a writer to be assigned to a composer's studio, if indeed she had been, and to debating the merits of the studio in

question itself, about which there was mixed opinion. It had
been recently redone, so that it had lost much of its turn-of-
the-century charm—a poet, Southern, easily twenty years older
than anyone else there, who had been coming to the Colony
"since y'all were hardly more than children," was lamenting
now—but it was larger than most of the other studios and had
a second story. Also it was farther out, at the end of the long-
est and most twisting road, which on the whole thought to be
a good thing (*Not to me*, declared the sculptor who'd made the
joke about pregnancy. *I'd be looking out for a goddamn cab*). There
was a fine piano, of course—which, somebody mentioned, was
nice for a writer if she happened to play, for who couldn't use
a bit of recreation around lunchtime?

Gad snorted. Nobody looked at him. He stood and
cleared his own place and left the dining room. He collected
his hat and coat, but kept the coat folded in his arms and instead of going out immediately, went round to the mailboxes;
he stopped there to put it on. While he buttoned the coat and
tied his scarf and pulled on his gloves, he casually checked the
names taped above all the boxes. There it was—they had already labeled a box for her: Hannah Something was Hannah
Sampas. He stared at it, surprised and pleased. This was at
least as good an omen as her lack of friends among those
present. Sampas was obviously Greek, simplified by immi-
gration authorities. And who but Jews named daughters
Hannah? That she was likely to be Greek and Jewish might
not necessarily give them a reason to be friends, but it did provide an opening conversational gambit that was more interesting than the tiresome questions *he'd* been greeted with on
his first evening, when he'd been tempted to offer to distrib-
ute copies of his c.v. instead of answering.

As he tramped through the snow in his unsuitable
boots, making his way to his studio deep in the woods—though
not as deep in as the one in which it had been suggested that
Hannah Sampas would be working—he embellished the im-

age of her he had already begun to conjure up: slight, with
dark hair, thickly curled, and dark eyes; an animated pretty
face, no makeup. He dressed her in jeans and velvet—a combination that had moved him since his sophomore year in high
school, courtesy of his first girlfriend, Victoria Brickner—and
began, experimentally, a conversation with her in his mind: he
spoke of his parents with affection and respect, in passing
mentioning the name of the Greek island where they both were
born; he referred to himself, with a wry grin, as the miracle
child of their middle age in the new world of the Bronx, U.S.
When it was her turn to talk, he bestowed upon her a Greek-
born father, somewhat younger than his own, and an Ameri-
can-born Jewish mother of—wild guess—Eastern European
parentage, Russian or Polish. They marveled over what they
had in common; compared differences.

Gad let himself speak of his work, though not at length
or in detail—*she* did not require an annotated list of works commissioned or performed—and when she spoke again, she told
him that she was a playwright (he hesitated here, but came to
this decision on the off-chance that she did teach in the midwest
and the even more remote chance that her job was at the same
midwestern college where his wife taught—for he knew that
if she happened to know Janet even slightly she would be dis-
posed to dislike him, since Janet complained about him to every woman she met, even those she barely knew. Partly this
was because she had plenty to complain about—he did not
deny that, not even to himself—but partly, Janet had admitted
once, it was to "inoculate" the women she met before *he* met
them. "So they'll be immune to your abundant charms," she'd
told him, and despite the sarcasm he'd understood her, for
she'd said for years that she despised the way he suddenly
became "compulsively seductive—Mr. Charming" when he
met a pretty woman. He had thought of asking her, when she'd
made her snide remark about inoculating all the women with
whom she came into contact first, why she bothered going to

the trouble of providing a list of his shortcomings to every member of her gender: why not pass over the ones who *weren't* pretty? But he didn't ask her this. Over the last few years, he had tried to sidestep trouble rather than taking a cheerful careless leap, the way he used to, into it; he'd tried to avoid the biggest arguments—the small, stupid, day-to-day ones were quite terrible enough).

He shivered, not just cold now—and his "boots," such as they were, were soaked through already—but depressed as well. Thinking about Janet always depressed him; he'd been trying not to do so since he'd left home. He hadn't called her, either, since he'd been here. Nor had she called him, though she had the number of the payphone just outside the dining room, which rang incessantly throughout breakfast and dinner every day. No doubt she was waiting for him to call first. The question of who had the upper hand at any given time (usually him, according to Janet) was ever uppermost in her mind. Besides, he had equivocated a bit when he'd left the number with her (as instructed in a letter from the Colony that also had suggested that he bring a pair of "tall, stout rubber boots" and a flashlight with extra batteries— "your sleepaway camp list," Janet had called it. "Would you like me to sew nametags into all your clothes?"); he had told her it was "for emergencies," which the letter hadn't said.

He knew he should call home—knew that it was dreadful of him, really, not to have done it yet—but if he did, he knew too, he would not be able to resist telling her how things stood here. He could never resist telling her when things went badly for him (it had more than once crossed his mind that this was his gift to her—the one gift he could give her freely: the chance for her to lord it over him, to enjoy his discomfort or humiliation). If he called her, she would end up sounding pleased, saying "I told you so," reminding him of the advice she'd given him two weeks ago as she drove him to the airport—a laundry list of instructions on how not to of-

fend anyone. His ill-advised speech, his second night in residence; his mentioning, in a kind of panic, when it became clear
that they were turning away from him, the *Times* roundup of
up-and-coming composers (a dire mistake, he'd realized, even
as he had begun to speak of it); his habit of retiring to his bedroom right after the evening's program, the reading or the slide
show or the screening of a video or film that he most often
dozed through anyway, to read for an hour or two one of the
books he'd brought before he went to sleep—instead of playing games or drinking himself blind (or both, as most of them
did) or squeezing along into someone's car like a teenager, roar-
ing out into the night in search of entertainment—in all of these
he had scrupulously ignored Janet's advice. "Don't set yourself apart. Don't come off superior. Don't brag. Don't try to
sell yourself. For God's sake don't say or do anything without
having thought about it first for a good fifteen minutes, and if
you have any doubts at all about how people might respond,
then don't say or do *anything*." Et cetera, et cetera.

   He had to remind himself now, as he often had to remind Janet, that he was not universally disliked, that he was
in possession of three of the most devoted friends that anyone
could have. He had retained one each, respectively, from childhood (P.S. 209), high school (Sheepshead), and college
(Wesleyan, where he'd also met Janet). And all of these trusted,
long-time friends were male (he liked to point this out to Janet,
in his own defense, when she claimed that he had no use for
men, that he was only interested in women). Unfortunately,
all three lived in New York—Magrisso and Antar had never
left, and Doolittle, who had grown up in Manchester, New
Hampshire, had ended up, strangely enough, teaching at
Brooklyn College—hundreds of miles from where he and Janet
were obliged to live, where, it was true, he had made no friends
in all these years. It was also true that he had no friends among
what Janet called his "peers." He hated that word. She had
urged him to get to know the composers who taught at the

University, and he had done that, to some extent; he had, at least, met each of them: three men, one much older than he and two a good bit younger, whom he found to be dull, complacent, humorless. What he'd told Janet was, "To know them slightly is to know them well." He ran into one or another of them from time to time on campus, in the halls or the Department office on the odd quarter when he taught, or at concerts at the Arts center, but they nodded at each other without speaking. It drove Janet crazy: she was certain that he needed "colleagues." He not only felt that he had no such need, but privately he wondered at Janet's commitment to the idea, since she had dozens, perhaps hundreds, of what she called colleagues, and it seemed to him they caused her no end of unhappiness. (It occurred to him suddenly that the flutter of excitement that had swept through him at breakfast, when it had seemed possible, just for an instant, that Hannah Sampas was a "colleague" of the kind that Janet was so sure he ought to cultivate, had not been born of his imagining that this would mark a great improvement in his circumstances here—that he had misconstrued the quickening of his own heart. It had not been hope at all, he thought, that he had felt; it had been dread.)

From what he could see, colleagues were full of spite and rivalry. *His* friends (Magrisso was a scientist, a chemist; Antar worked in all-news radio; Doolittle taught Russian) loved him unreservedly and took nothing but pleasure in each of his well-spaced triumphs; they were full of genuine sorrow and sympathy, too, when he had a disappointment. All three of them had called him by ten-thirty on the Saturday night that the next day's Sunday *Times* had come out with its piece about composers under forty, to congratulate him and to rail at the *Times* for the position he'd been given on their list (number twenty-eight out of the thirty-three) and for the measly two lines they'd devoted to him. It was thanks to his friends in New York that he heard about the piece before seeing it; he'd known it was coming, naturally, but he hadn't known the ar-

ticle would take the form of a ranked list—nor that the brief
description of him would include a sentence that still galled
him, although months had passed. Doolittle, who'd been the
first to call, had read him the whole article over the phone,
and after he had read the second sentence—"Gadol is by far
the brashest, the loosest cannon of the bunch: he may well either explode on the scene or blow off prematurely"—which
almost completely undermined the effect of the first, flatter-
ing one about his "bold, even brave risk-taking, his wit and
scope and depth as he flies in the face of the 'truths' most contemporary composers accept on faith," Doolittle paused to mut-
ter, "Jerkoff—two-bit, no-nothing reporter. Who the goddamn
hell does he think *he* is?" before moving on to number twenty-
nine. Gad was grateful—grateful both that Doolittle had acknowledged the crumminess of this, and that he didn't make
a bigger deal of it. When the others called, to crow for him
and tell him that they'd always known he'd be a star, they did
likewise—made passing remarks on the *Times* writer's insuffi-
cient faculties and cursed the list itself, Gad's place on it, and
both the paucity and idiocy of what had been said about him.

About the somber fact that Gad would cease to be
under forty on the very day that Sunday *Times* was dated (a
fact about which Janet saw fit, the next morning when he went
out to pick up their own copy of the paper, to make jokes), not
one of his friends said a word. All three simply called *again*,
on Sunday afternoon, to wish him a happy birthday. *That* was
friendship. Why on God's earth would he have any need for
the sort of "friends" Janet had, and wished for him?

Of course, that didn't mean he was incapable of feeling excluded—or that his feelings couldn't be hurt. On his
very first night *here*, as he'd sat on the couch watching the pa-
rade of artists troop in stamping snow off their stout rubber
boots, surrendering ski poles and peeling off layers of clothes
and tossing them into one huge intimate pile by the door, laughing and shouting to each other, for fifteen minutes no one spoke

to him or looked in his direction—and when finally a skinny, nervous-looking fellow sank down next to him and Gad opened his mouth to speak to him, the fellow held up his left hand and said, "No, no, don't bother. I'm leaving in the morning. Getting to know me would be a waste of time."

At first he'd thought the trouble was that he had never been to such a place before—that the others knew the ropes, that there was some code of behavior that he wasn't privy to. But it wasn't long before he found out that a number of the other guests, or residents—or, as the staff here called them, colonists (which amused him; it made them sound like a band of Crusoes having claimed their island)—had never been in residence here or at another colony before. Five people seated at his table on his second night at dinner—the night he'd made his unfortunate speech—confessed to being first-timers. They were the ones who had the grace to look ashamed when he remarked that it seemed a grave sin to take this place for granted, to gossip about each newcomer as if they were at a party; to act as if it were their *due* to have lunch brought to their doors silently, with such grave reverence for what it was assumed was going on behind those doors, by an old man in coveralls and a plaid hunting cap with earflaps; to pretend that there was nothing marvelous about not having to cook dinner for themselves, or wash the dishes afterwards (Janet and he took turns: one cooked, one washed, on alternate nights), or go shopping for the groceries required to cook those dinners and unpack the bags into the kitchen cabinets and the refrigerator (all of which he and Janet did together, Saturdays), or shovel snow or scrub the bathtub or replace a burnt-out light bulb.

But all of them had been there for at least a week, and even *they* had grown accustomed to the place by then; no one went so far as to agree with him. And when he was finished (when, to be precise, he made himself shut up), one fellow— one of those tall, beefy-looking sculptors, who had been in residence for three weeks and would be there for another five (the one who, Gad had already been informed, lived year-round at colonies, traveling from one to another, so that, it was rumored, he had even ceased to have gas and electric service in his New York apartment and had given up his share of a studio in Chinatown), and who had a reputation, Gad had since then overheard, for having bedded all three of the single women in attendance—barked out a harsh laugh, then murmured, "Pompous asshole."

No, it wasn't just that he was new to this world. Now he'd been here long enough, if it were in his nature, to be "used to it," to fit in. But he would never fit in—it was his nature not to. He was a misfit. That was really what it came down to: to misfitting, and being chronically misunderstood.

He made his way down the last road that led to his little cabin. He could see it poking up out of the snow just over a small hill, and the sight of it cheered him, as it did every morning. Once he was inside it, he knew, he'd feel better still. Simply being in the studio, with all the hours of the day ahead and no possibility of being disturbed, was so pleasurable to him that all gloom, all self-pity, all disquieting thoughts were banished.

Besides, he was freezing. His hiking boots, which he'd had since grad school—and in which he'd never actually gone hiking (in which, for that matter, he'd done very little walking, since he'd been living, all these years, in places in which no one did much walking: there was nothing to walk *to*)—his poor unsuitable, ancient, just-over-the-ankle hiking boots were useless here. And above them, all the way up to his knees, his jeans were soaked—his punishment for each time he had inattentively wandered or stumbled for a step or two off the narrow path that had been cleared, and into the banks of snow on either side of it. Had he attended to the advice in the letter from the Colony, his feet, his socks, his jeans up to his knees would all be dry. But the list had seemed so *precious*. He wasn't going camping, after all, he'd told himself, and crumpled up the letter, disregarding all of its suggestions but the one about leaving the number of the payphone with someone at home in case he was "needed." But then the letter hadn't specifically mentioned that the Colony would be blanketed by several feet of snow in early April.

On the cabin's wooden porch, he stomped snow off his boots and jeans. Inside, he took off the boots, and then his coat and hat and gloves and scarf, and finally the jeans too, and his wet socks. Shivering in his undershorts and workshirt and wool cardigan, he fetched the sweatpants he'd kept on a hook beside the fireplace since his second day here, and the pair of socks he'd hung to dry yesterday morning on the fireplace screen.

He cranked up the thermostat (temporarily, he promised himself—just until he could get a good fire going) and as he built the fire, he admired his skill. It had taken most of his first week, and one near-disaster (the first day, when he'd forgotten—well, he'd never known—to open the flue), before he'd worked out just how this was done. Now he was an expert. He rubbed his palms together, watching the fire race across the kindling. Next in the set of rituals he performed each morning was to make a cup of tea. He filled a cup with tap water from the tiny bathroom sink and plugged in the immersion heater, dropped it in the cup. While he waited for the water to heat up, he searched the pockets of his sweater for teabags.

Finally he was at the piano—warm and dry, a cup of Lemon Zinger in his hand. He looked around him. There was nothing much to the one-room cabin: a little desk under the window, and a wooden swivel chair that looked uncomfortable—he never sat in it; an armchair, with a small, square side table beside it, where he read while he ate the two sandwiches, the carrot sticks, the apple, and the cookie that were left for him each day at noon in the black metal lunchbox; the cot on which he napped for twenty minutes daily after lunch; a hooked rug, two bookcases, the fireplace tools, a wastebasket. A few scattered lamps. The curtained-off, cramped bathroom. The piano. His own books and papers, pens and pencils, two as-yet unopened packages of good-quality manuscript paper, stacks of cassette tapes and spiral-bound pads and the yellow nine-stave cards that he was partial to, scrawled on and fanned out everywhere around the room. A small portable stereo. No computer—he had not learned how to use one and had no interest in doing so (despite the *Times* reporter who'd considered this such a peculiarity, and came back to it at least three times in his interview, which naturally Gad had assumed would be printed, if not in its entirety then at least in *part*).

He sipped his tea as he took in all that surrounded him. It seemed to him that what was in this room was all he needed in the world, and for a moment he almost understood the sculptor who never went home—what the hell was his name, anyway: Kurtz? Kotz? Of course, that was extreme. Still, he should have done this long ago, he told himself.

But then he hadn't had the choice. On the two or three occasions he had brought it up over the years, Janet had raised one eyebrow and smiled sardonically. "An artists' colony? Ah, you mean a place where you get to spend a month or two away from home—away from *me*—sleeping under the same roof with perhaps two dozen other exquisitely sensitive people, roughly half of them women, who've left *their* homes along with whatever minimal commitments and poorly understood responsibilities bind them to the real world? You're joking, right?" Once—long ago—he'd said, "It's not Sodom and Gomorrah, you know. It's just a place where artists go to get some work done." But this had made her angry. "Don't talk to me as if I were a moron," she'd told him. "I know exactly what an artists' colony is." And calmly: "That's why I know you must be joking."

Well, she'd mistrusted him; he understood that. And she'd had good reason to. Or she'd once had good reason to—

more than two years had passed since she'd last had one. If she had consented to his going now, it was in part because this time he'd simply filled out and sent in the application without speaking of it first, and maintained his silence until he had been accepted—"invited" was the way the Colony's form letter phrased it—so that he'd presented her not with an idea, as he'd done before, but a solid offer of six weeks in spring (a fait accompli, she had called it, and he'd said, "Why not look at it, instead, as an honor they're bestowing on me? They could just as easily have rejected my application"), but it was mostly, he knew, because two years had passed by then since he had sworn, or resworn, his fidelity to her—and he had made good on his promise, and she knew it.

What she didn't know was what had been behind the oath he'd taken. The truth was he'd grown tired himself of his. . .well, he had never been sure what to call them. His affairs, Janet would say, or his romances (both words had the scent of melodrama, which was why he disliked them; naturally, they were the words that Janet chose to use). *Relationships* was sterile-sounding, modern and efficient in a way that didn't seem to him at all to describe the process of persuading himself that he was in love—or at least sufficiently in love to take the steps that led to an entanglement (now there was a much better word!) with yet another obviously imperfect woman—then realizing, after a few weeks or months, that he had misled himself, and her—whomever she was this time— once again. The women he became entangled with nearly always called this mishap a "relationship." In any case, the whole cycle—which had become so dismally predictable—of elation, disappointment, sorrow, and recrimination (which itself became a bore, and out of boredom he would find himself casting about *again*: a restless period between "affairs" which amounted to the only time he could get any work done) had begun to weary and at last depress him just as much as his marriage did.

And actually it had been easier than he'd expected to "stay out of trouble" (Janet's warning phrase). It wasn't as if he were so good-looking or so obviously, effortlessly magnetic that he had to fight women off. His appeal, he knew—knew, mostly, because Janet had explained it to him—was something he himself controlled, so that when he chose to, he became attractive. He wasn't bad-looking, Janet said; nor was he uninteresting. But when he wanted to win someone over it was just as if he had a switch he could throw.

And she insisted that she always knew when he had thrown it—which was how, she said, she knew that he'd "been good" for so long. "You turn yourself on but you can't turn yourself off," was what she told him, finally explaining how she'd always seemed to know when he had been unfaithful. "You stay on until you burn out"—so that whenever he was in the process of falling in love with someone new, she said, he became "idiotically charming" even at home, to her. Thus she knew he'd kept his word. "Think back," she said. "Can you recall—*I* can't—the last time you were even remotely pleasant to me?"

If she knew that he had given up his infidelities because they were more trouble than they turned out to be worth—because, he had discovered as the weeks and months passed, that his own needs had been reduced until they seemed to have vanished—would she have been less pleased with him? Less likely to have let him go, now, to the Colony? *She* seemed to have no need for love, or even for tenderness. Was that possible? As far as he knew, she'd been faithful to him all along. Perhaps he'd reached the point at which she had been from the start—a place where no longing existed, where love was itself unimaginable.

So now she trusted him; she'd let him go. Still, she had proffered a scribbled in, dog-eared, and Post-It-noted paperback Bible—which she had handy, as she was teaching it that term in a seminar that looked at it as literature along with the Tao Te Ching, the Veda, the Avesta, the Koran, and the Old Norse Eddas—and made him swear on it (laughing, as if it really were a joke) that he would not use these six weeks away to renew his (more laughter, more pretense) "former evil ways."

This had been particularly easy. Indeed, Janet would have been amused if she had known he would be living among such spectacularly unbeautiful examples of her gender. The four women who had been in residence when he'd first arrived were so plain he'd been truly shocked when he'd heard that that sculptor, Kotz or Katz or Kurtz, between sessions with twisted steel and molten lead, had slept with all but the married novelist among them. Three of that group were gone now, including the married novelist, but they'd been replaced, over the last nine or ten days, by five equally ill-favored women (the sculptor, Gad had overheard, had made his way through two of them already). The one remaining woman from the original group was a pathologically shy, thirtyish poet—Gad had never heard her speak above a whisper—who wore her hair in a wispy pale brown bun that she was forever patting, and who was both so thin and so frightened looking he had sometimes imagined she was about to fall into a faint. He'd felt rather sorry for her since it had become clear that the sculptor had lost interest in her, and out of sympathy he'd tried once to engage her in a conversation while they waited for the dinner bell, but she had blinked her oversized eyes and turned away without even bothering to whisper a response.

It was she, in fact, who was present in the otherwise empty commons room when Gad returned to it that evening after what had turned out to be an exceptionally good day—a good enough day so that he had felt at ease knocking off nearly a full hour earlier than usual. He nodded at her when she glanced up from the *Times* to see who'd just come in, and although she tightened her lips—perhaps she even frowned—at least she nodded back. He smiled at her then; why not? His mood was excellent. As of today, the sinfonietta was finished—

finished! Which meant that tomorrow, with four weeks of his
residency still to go, he would begin on the concerto, which he
had told himself before he'd left home he might start to *think*
about if there was time, knowing that this was a bit of foolish
optimism: he had never worked that quickly, that efficiently,
that *well*. Indeed, he'd had no idea how much he could accomplish in so short a time, freed for once of all the usual dis-
tractions of his ordinary life: answering the phone and taking
messages for Janet, returning calls that she had taken messages
about for him, opening the bills that came in each day's mail
and stacking them in order of their urgency, arguing with Janet
over whose turn it was that month to sit down and actually
pay them, taking out the trash and going to the bank and standing squinting up at leaf- and twig-filled rain gutters and wondering if he ought to be doing something about them,
putting gas in their dilapidated Duster and making sure the
car was "running right" (a command of Janet's that he'd never
understood, and about which he did nothing much more
than to worry, silently and out loud both, which evidently
was sufficient).

His smile took the poet by surprise, and that pleased
him so much that as the others straggled in over the next three-
quarters of an hour, he smiled at every one of them. It surprised them all, he saw. They disliked him; they expected to
be disliked in return. And usually he was glad to oblige. But
tonight he found that it was very pleasant to catch them off
guard. Besides, he *felt* like smiling. In a fit of benevolence, he
even wished them all the sort of day he had just had—he
wished them all a *string* of such good days. He had good will
to spare. And he had a feeling, too, that something interesting
and even delightful was about to happen.

Thus he kept smiling and nodding, for all the world
like the host of a grand party, from the spot he'd staked out by
the door—the very door through which, at any moment, the
new person, Hannah Sampas, would appear.

And then there she was. He allowed her fifteen seconds to stand uncertainly, unnoticed by the others, in the entryway, but as she pulled the stocking cap from her head, releasing an abundance of dark curls, he leapt up from the armchair. Startled—she even took a step back toward the door—then grateful, Gad observed approvingly, when he came forward, singing out (though softly, in no hurry to alert the others), "Good evening! Good evening! Welcome!"—exactly as he had wished someone had on his first night—she took off her mittens (which, like the tasseled, foot-long stocking cap, were striped: pink, turquoise, yellow, and magenta), stuffed them into the side pockets of her puffy, many-pocketed and multi-zippered pale blue jacket, and grasped the hand he offered. "Thank you," she said. "I'm Hannah Sampas."

"Demetrius Gadol."

He noted that there was a ring on every finger of the hand that he was shaking; also that the mittens had not done her any good: the bands of silver and the colored stones with which they were generously studded were so cold against his own skin that he flinched—then tried to make up for it by covering their joined hands for an instant with his left hand. It was not until then that she smiled, and only then—as if the smile had raised a curtain—did he see how very pretty she was. Much prettier, he thought, than he'd been able (or dared?) to imagine.

He released her hand—which, he took note, was no bigger than a child's. Fleetingly—inescapably—he thought of Janet, whose hands (bare, always, of all jewelry: she wore both her wedding ring and watch—which, explaining that she liked to keep her wrists "unfettered," she had liberated from its band the day after he'd bought it for her, nearly twenty years ago—on a chain around her neck, along with the heart-shaped locket that had been her grandmother's), were slightly larger than his own; only slightly, and yet still enough so that he was aware of it. Just as he was aware that she was not quite an inch taller

than he was. Next to Janet, he thought, Hannah Sampas—
was she even five feet tall?—would look like a child. Indeed,
even standing by herself before him, and despite (perhaps in
part because of?) the big, complicated-looking sky blue jacket,
with its padding and its puffed-out pockets and its many fas-
tenings and flaps, she looked not just slight but *small*.

She tugged at its central zipper now, and shrugged
the jacket off. "Demetrius Gadol," she said. "An interesting
name." And apparently she meant this, for she closed
her eyes and cocked her head—her brow creased, lips
pursed: thinking hard, it seemed. About his name? He was
absurdly flattered.

He watched her think. He took advantage of the opportunity to examine her, and he was struck by how close a
match she was in the flesh to the Hannah he'd allowed himself to conjure: slight, in tomboy clothes (no velvet, but that
had been a frill); black curls around her face, brushing her
shoulders, fanning out around her—a great untamed mass of
hair through which peeked bits of silver: dangling earrings,
many tiers' worth. Within the collar of her red-and-black
checked flannel shirt a string of tiny dark red beads—they
looked like pomegranate seeds—gleamed. He thought of the
discreet gold studs his wife wore in her earlobes; the thick gold
chain she wore around her neck. He thought of Janet asking
him, so long ago, how much he "minded" her hanging her
wedding band alongside her grandmother's locket and the
watch he'd given her the year before, when she'd turned
twenty-one ("I just can't wear a ring," she'd told him, "I never
have. I just can't bear the thought of anything on my hands").
He glanced at Hannah Sampas's left hand and saw that she
wore four rings on it, too (which made his mouth twitch: Janet
mocked such women; called them "magpies"), but the ring on
the third finger, an elaborate silver butterfly with tiny gold
and green stones scattered liberally across its wings, was not—
surely not—a wedding band.

"My friends call me Gad," he said.

At this, Hannah burst out laughing. Gad took a step back, unnerved, but before he could form a question, or Hannah could offer an explanation, the dinner bell rang.

"Intermission's over?" she said.

"Dinner," he said stiffly.

It was not until they started toward the dining room that it occurred to him that they were being watched: a path seemed to have been made for them so that they were obliged to go in first. Walking the gauntlet, Gad thought. But he kept his expression blank; he could only hope Hannah would do the same.

In the dining room he panicked. What he would have given for a table set for two! As it was, since they'd been forced to come in first, he couldn't even choose among the least of all the evils for their tablemates. He foresaw the worst. But as there was nothing to be done, he gestured (grandly, he hoped) to the roomful of long, empty tables and said, "You choose."

As they sat down she leaned toward him and whispered, "My *cat* is called Gad."

"Your cat is what?" he said.

She was laughing again. This time he laughed too, his eyes on her. If her smile had raised a curtain, he thought, then her laugh—a laugh in which true happiness was manifest— was pure illumination. You'd have to be made of stone to resist the pull, the lure, of such unequivocal, sincere delight. "Your cat? No!" he said merrily, and realized as he said it that he didn't even mind that Hannah *had* a cat, though this was an especial and longstanding prejudice of his. Of his and Janet's. It was one of the few things they still agreed on: animal ownership itself suggested desperation and self-delusion, and those who kept cats—animals that were "the embodiment," as Janet put it, "of denuded ferity" (not to mention how repellent Gad found their disdainful, cold, self-serving brand of sensuality)— were the most delusional and most pathetic of all pet owners.

He and Janet had discovered this shared vehemence the night they had first met—it was one of the subjects of their first (and fateful, for it ended in his dorm room) conversation: Janet, telling him about her home town and her childhood, spoke with detectable bitterness of a household in which multiple pets were always kept (birds, fish, dogs, cats, white mice, box turtles and guinea pigs; her elder sisters and her mother had particularly adored the cats, of which there had been a long series, in particular); Gad, an only child, had grown up with his mother's much beloved pair of cats, and he confessed to having often wished them dead (so that when they *had* at last expired, in his middle-teens—one quickly following the other, the second one "of nothing more fatal than grief," his mother said—he had felt just as guilty as relieved).

"I didn't *name* her Gad," said Hannah. "I mean, I didn't name her that on purpose. She's really The Magnificent Gadfly. But obviously that's not what you call out when you're trying to coax her up into your lap. I'd imagined that I'd call her Maggie for short, but you know how it is with names. You never can tell what'll stick. She's been Gad from the beginning, and that's eight years now, so she's got dibs."

"I've had the name longer than that," he said. "I'm the one with dibs on it."

"Not as far as I'm concerned," Hannah told him. "I'll have to call you something else." She tapped her chin with her right index finger. "No one calls you Demetrius?"

"Only my wife," Gad said glumly, and with this—as if by speaking of her he had called Janet's astral spirit to join them—his mood shifted and settled. He fixed his eyes on the ring that circled Hannah's index finger: a broad silver band set with a square blue-gray stone—the color of the ocean where it darkens, at the place it starts to get deep. He didn't want to meet her eyes now, not until he'd banished that judgmental apparition.

"No one else? What about your parents?"

"They have their own name for me."

"Which is?"

"It's a Ladino nickname."

"And what would that be?"

"Ladino? It's the language of—"

"No," Hannah said. "I mean, what's the nickname?"

Despite himself, he began to laugh. "You think I know you well enough for that?" And when she looked disappointed—which was sweet, he thought: sweet enough to chase away the grim and unforgiving specter of his wife—he added, "Understand, please, that there isn't *anyone* I know well enough for that. Don't take it personally."

"I take everything personally. It's my job."

He was about to ask what job that was exactly when Hannah nudged him and inclined her head. Their table had filled. Gad was not the least surprised to look around and find that if he'd made a list of everyone he wished most to avoid, he could have checked off all the names by glancing at his dinner partners. Of course, he first would have had to *learn* their names: he discovered now, as he attempted to make introductions, that having had so little contact with them, there was not one name about which he was absolutely certain. The sculptor who'd had all of his utilities shut off (the one who had called Gad a pompous asshole and who now had the temerity to sit, smirking, across the table from him) was called Keech, he learned, not Kotz or Kurtz. His first name—which Gad was sure he'd never heard before—was Alfred. The unstable-looking poet with the schoolmarm bun and eyes like saucers (who had edged into the seat beside the sculptor, who ignored her) was Doreen Fitzgibbon; Gad had introduced her as Eileen Fitzgerald. And the "light artist," who'd beaten Keech the sculptor to the seat on Hannah's left, was not (Gad's guess, by this time without hope) Marco Mezzoli but "alas," said he, "Antonio Azzoli." After these three failures, Gad gave up and let the others introduce themselves.

Hannah nodded; she repeated names. With each name she gave out a low-watt version of her smile. Gad waited impatiently; he was growing irritable. None of them, it seemed, could utter his or her own name and leave it at that. Vitae were presented; Hannah's was demanded.

But it wasn't long before he ceased to be annoyed—before he realized that thanks to the artless questions of the others at the table, he was learning much that was of interest to him. In rapid order, then, he found out that she lived in New York, in the Village; that she supported herself by teaching part-time at three, sometimes four, different colleges; that she had not only grown up in New York but had gone to college and to graduate school there—that she had never lived anywhere else, but for a single academic quarter last year, when she'd taught somewhere in Kansas (which cleared up the mystery of "the middle of nowhere"); that her first book had come out last year and won a prize; that the prize was for a first book by a poet under thirty.

That she was a poet was a disappointment to him. His experience with poets had been uniformly bad. Janet knew a number of them; he'd been to their parties and they'd been to Janet's (he had never thought of Janet's parties as in any way *his*). Forced to socialize with them, he'd found them dull, depressing company. (And then, of course, there was his experience *here*, which had not challenged any of his expectations.) But so far, he reminded himself, Hannah had been neither dull nor in the least depressing. She was perhaps the exception among poets—she was charming. And as if to prove this to him now, she turned to him—away from the light artist, though *he* was still talking—and said, softly, "So, besides my cat's name and the name only your wife calls you by and the name only your parents call you by, what are my options?"

"The sky's the limit," he said. He felt cheerful again now. "You go ahead and just invent your own name for me, anything you please."

She actually seemed to be taking this offer to heart. She was silent, and he watched the square ocean-colored stone move as she tapped her finger to her lips. "All right," she said finally. "But you'll have to give me a few days. I need to get to know you before I can name you."

"Take your time. I shall remain nameless as long as necessary."

"That's very gallant of you."

He grinned; he blushed.

"So," she said. "Here's something curious."

"What's that?"

"You're the lone soul at this table whose vocation is a secret to me."

Was it his imagination, or was she was mocking the others?

"It's no secret at all," he said. "I simply haven't had the chance to tell you that."

"Nor anything else about yourself."

"Such as?"

"Where you teach. *If* you teach. Where you live." She lowered her voice and leaned toward him so that only he could hear her. "What you've *done*. What you've won. Who you know."

Gad grinned at her again.

She grinned back. The all-out version this time.

And as they started on their meal (some kind of stew, as usual, and overcooked white rice and salad), he began to tell her everything that he had planned to tell her. By the time dessert (a type of pudding—butterscotch? banana? Sometimes Gad thought the mystery associated with the food they were served here was quite intentional—was a sort of joke perpetuated on them by the staff; the quality of what was served, too, seemed to him a joke, perhaps meant to tell them that to the staff waiting on them they were inmates of an institution, that "colonists" was a bureaucratic euphemism) had been brought

to the tables, Hannah had begun *her* story, which turned out to
be so like what Gad had imagined for her that he thumped the
table with his fist. "I knew it!" he cried when she told him that
she was both Greek and Jewish, the product of just such a
marriage as he had envisioned (although the details differed:
both parents were first-generation, both Bronx-born—like himself! he interjected—and it was her father's parents, who were
not much older than Gad's parents, who were Greek-born; it
was her grandfather whose name had been changed on arrival). And her mother's parents? Gad asked. One Polish-
born, one Russian-born—he had hit the mark on that exactly.

As they talked, Gad nearly managed once more to forget the presence of the others. Their tablemates, for their part,
seemed to have lost interest in Hannah. Certainly she was
spending too much time talking to *him* to remain of interest to
them, and talking (and with too much pleasure, irony-free)
about things that didn't interest them at all. What *did*—besides grants, prizes, and reviews in the *Times Book Review* or in
the art pages of Friday's *Times* or in *Art in America*—Gad had
no idea. He didn't care. Indeed, he so profoundly didn't care
that it was only now that he realized that he *had* cared before.
It had driven him mad, hadn't it, to sit among them at breakfast on Sunday mornings listening as the writers speculated
about which reviewers owed favors to—or else must be sleeping with—the novelists to whom they'd given good reviews
(likewise, which bad reviews were the result of grudges held:
professional, sexual, or otherwise)? It had driven him mad—
why not admit it to himself?—that they'd dismissed him. Was
there anything about them that had *not* infuriated him? And
yet now, as he and Hannah, finished with their meal, stood up
and began to clear their dishes, he wasn't even irritated when
Keech (Albert? Alfred?) the obnoxious sculptor called out, "Oh,
no! Going so soon?" And then when Hannah paused to turn
back and say, sweetly, "It was so nice to meet all of you—see
you tomorrow" (she actually waved at them, like a child say-

ing goodbye to the group she'd fallen in with on the playground), he laughed out loud and waved goodbye himself.

They were the first to wander from the dining room into the commons room—still talking steadily. They drifted through the room. They had just made the discovery that the Bronx neighborhood where Gad's parents had lived when they had first come to America from Greece—the neighborhood where Gad was born, where he had lived until he turned five—was where Hannah's father had grown up. He was caught off balance by this for an instant, for it made the ten-year difference between Hannah and himself (ten years nearly the day, they had discovered, for their birthdays were a week apart) seem more like a generation, but Hannah was already on to something else—her own childhood in Brooklyn—and he was so entranced by this additional coincidence, it banished his discomfort before it had secured a foothold. "I was raised in Brooklyn *too*," he interrupted her. "That was *where* we moved when I was five!" They laughed; they agreed that this was amazing.

That they had lived at practically the opposite ends of the borough and had never once ventured into each other's neighborhoods didn't mitigate their pleasure. They exchanged tales of their "escapes"—Gad's over twenty years ago, for college (and because soon after he had left, his parents had left too, for Florida, and the two friends he had retained from childhood had both fled the neighborhood, Magrisso to the West Side of Manhattan and Antar to Chelsea, it had been so long now since he'd last set foot in Sheepshead Bay he couldn't say *when* that had been); Hannah's just eight years ago, since she'd lived with her parents in East Flatbush all through Brooklyn College. Because her parents *still* lived there, she had to go back too often to have turned even half-jokingly nostalgic, the way Gad could be about the chain-link fenced-in triangular "play area" outside their apartment building on Avenue Z, or Grand's five-and-dime on Sheepshead Bay Road, where he'd

bought toy cigarettes that puffed out clouds of talcum powder, or the school plays he had always sung the leads in—"the
Maestro" in third grade's "The Lost Note," Don José in the
fifth grade version of "Carmen"—or dodge ball or Spud in the
schoolyard at P.S. 209.

Hannah had to walk by her old elementary school each
time she went "home"—it was halfway between the subway
stop and her parents' house—and she groaned when he waxed
poetic about his. "It's too easy to get sentimental when you're
a thousand miles away."

"Five hundred miles."

She waved away the difference. "*I'm* just across the
damn river."

"Which I'd love to be, myself."

They were standing now almost exactly where they
had stood talking before the dinner bell had rung. They smiled
at each other. "Do you really miss New York?" she said. "Lately
I've been thinking that it's time to get out of there."

"Because you're too near your family?"

"No, not because of that. Because. . .I don't know.
Because I have to teach part-time at four different schools to
earn a living. Because I've been living in a one-room apartment in the Village for eight years and when I look at the apartment listings in the *Voice* I might as well be reading random
passages of a Gothic romance for all the practical application
they have to my life."

Gad clucked sympathetically. His friend Magrisso's
place on the Upper West Side, he told her, had long been too
small for him and the wife he had acquired five years ago.
"He says no one moves in New York anymore. *He* reads the
Sunday Times real estate ads for a laugh—he says they're better
than the Sunday comics in the *News*. But his wife would cut
off her right arm for one more closet."

"I don't even have a closet," Hannah said. "I hang my
clothes, six or seven hangers deep, on three-inch nails across

the wall above my bed. Which is across the room from my kitchen table. Which is beside my bathtub. And if anyone moved in with *me*, one of us would have to get up *on* the bed or climb into the bathtub to make room for the other to turn around."

"At least you don't have a roommate. Magrisso had a roommate before he got married. It was the only way he could afford his place. And my friend Antar had a series of roommates before *he* got married."

"I couldn't bear to have a roommate. I've never had one; I can't even imagine it."

"So you've always lived alone, since you left your parents' house?" Gad tried to imagine *this*—but how could he? He had never lived alone. First there had been his parents, then a roommate, briefly, and then Janet. Janet for so many years.

"Alone except for the other Gad."

Ah—the other Gad. He had forgotten all about his namesake.

Politely, then—for he remembered how his mother had been about *her* cats—he asked, "Who's taking care of it—her, is it?—while you're here?" When he was growing up they'd never taken a vacation because his mother was convinced that there was no one she could trust with her cats.

"My. . .I guess you'd call him my fiancé. But it's interesting that you should ask. I've been worrying since the second I got on the bus today. We've never been apart before for more than a few days, when I could just leave out a lot of food and water and tell myself she wouldn't notice I was gone much longer than I might be to teach, say—I mean, can a cat tell that one day is over and another has begun? But this is something else. She's not even *home*. I had to bring her to his apartment. And he's not that crazy about cats. Plus I know he doesn't take seriously just how dependent—really, how totally dependent—on me Gad *is*."

The human Gad considered this. He actually took Janet's advice for once and thought before he spoke. He even ran through a number of possible responses before he settled on the noncommittal, "Fiancé?"

"John," said Hannah. "Although I call him Saint John. Which he hates."

"You have a good reason, I suppose," he asked her carefully, "to call him by a name he hates?"

"Oh, mostly to tease him," Hannah said. "But it happens also to be accurate."

"Oh?" Gad paused in the midst of buttoning his coat. He looked at her. She was smiling at him again. *Up* at him. This both pleased and unnerved him, a conflation of emotions that reminded him of something, but before he had a chance to think of what, she went on.

"He's a lawyer—which doesn't sound that virtuous, I know, but he does *pro bono* work in his spare time for practically his whole neighborhood on the Lower East Side. He *lives* on the Lower East Side, which he doesn't have to do. I mean, he has a decent enough job. He's an Assistant D.A. And when he's not at his job or working for free for his neighbors, he volunteers at Amnesty International, he's a Big Brother, *and* he makes home visits to people with AIDS. He gives them legal advice and brings them groceries and then he'll even cook and sit with—"

"All right, all right." Gad held up a hand to stop her. "I'm convinced." But he couldn't resist adding: "And who's taking care of this paragon in your absence?"

For a second she looked perplexed; then she laughed— wickedly, he thought; surprisingly. "Saint John takes care of himself. He's utterly self-sufficient."

"Really," Gad said.

"Really."

"A 'totally dependent' cat and an 'utterly independent' boyfriend—I'm sorry, fiancé? Are you sure you don't have your loved ones mixed up?"

"Alas, no," Hannah said. "That's the irony of my situation."

She was smiling up at him again. She'd put on her preposterous hat and now she threaded her arms into the sleeves of her jacket. The zipping and snapping and Velcro-fastening of flaps and tying of cords took a long time. Gad felt as if he ought to offer to help—the way one would offer to help a child getting dressed to go out and play in the snow. And truly, he thought, that was how she looked. She even had on the sort of knee-high rubber boots the staff had recommended. Hers were yellow; they made her look especially childlike. She looked, in fact, as if she could be lifted without any effort—as if, with both hands on her waist (the fingers meeting easily behind her, Gad suspected), one might simply lift her straight up in the air.

Those boots, that foot-long multicolored hat, those mittens hanging from her pockets like the striped tongues of two floppy stuffed toy dogs. That ridiculous jacket! And that smile of hers, he thought—that guileless, artlessly charming smile. That smile that was so frankly happy. Why—it only now occurred to him—her happiness itself. *Happiness*.

Contemplating this, *her*, himself unsmiling, in his long black coat, his black felt hat and black suede gloves, his white silk scarf crossed at his neck, he once more had the feeling that there was a generation between them—an uncrossable gulf.

His throat felt dry and for a moment he believed he couldn't, or wouldn't, speak. But it seemed to him a matter of some urgency that he overcome this. Abruptly, even harshly—so it seemed to his own ear—he asked her if she'd seen her studio and what she'd thought of it.

She hadn't seen it. She'd started out toward the studio shortly after she'd arrived this afternoon, she said, but she'd turned back after ten minutes and instead took a walk around the center of the Colony till dinnertime.

And why was that? he asked. Politely. Still feeling the chill of distance.

She blushed. "It's too stupid," she said. "You won't think less of me? You have to promise."

He promised. She hadn't even heard (had chosen not to hear?) the roughness in his voice, he thought.

She hadn't understood, she said, when she'd looked at the mimeographed map she had been given in the office upon checking in, just how far out her cabin was. She had not imagined it would take more than ten minutes to get there, and when she'd walked that long and saw that, based on the map, she had not yet reached the halfway point, she'd become uneasy. It struck her that venturing into the woods alone so late in the afternoon might not be such a good idea. "What if I lost my way and it started getting dark? That's what I had in my mind. I couldn't get past this awful vision of getting lost and a search party having to be sent out for me. The possibility was just too humiliating. I figured that tomorrow I'd start out early in the morning and I'd have all day to find it. It could be my first day's work." She lowered her voice: "I have *no* experience with woods."

Nor had he, he said with a sigh of what he recognized (did she? he wondered) as relief, as the gap that he'd imagined between them closed up. He added that he had, however, by now grown accustomed to these particular woods and would gladly take her to her studio if she liked.

"Now?" she said. "In the dark?"

He hadn't given any thought to how dark it would be now. And the only times he'd had cause to walk through the woods at night, there'd been a whole group going, heading out to someone's "open studio," with so many flashlights it might just as well have been midafternoon. But Hannah sounded so excited, he couldn't bring himself to retract what she'd clearly taken as an offer to start out immediately. "If you have a flashlight, sure."

"Of course I do," she said, and reached into one of her many pockets to produce it. "It was on the list."

They set out for her studio in a light snow. The moon was nearly full, and its light was so bright on the snow beneath their feet that it wasn't half as dark as he had feared. Hannah commented that it was brighter now, here, than it had been at noon in the city. "I thought the day itself was a bad omen for me; I could have sworn the sky was telling me something. It was so dim and colorless when I left town. 'A gray day. A heartless day,'" she said in a tone that made him wonder if she were quoting from a poem. "But *this*"—she drew her mittened hand in a wide arc—"this seems like a promise, doesn't it? It's like a dream. Or. . .I don't know, an illustration in a fine edition of Grimm's."

Amused, Gad said, "Should we leave breadcrumbs then, as we walk through it?"

"Certainly not," Hannah told him. "Pebbles. Otherwise we'll be defeated by the birds and we'll never find our way back."

Dutifully, Gad stopped and knelt to look for stones. "It's no use," he said. "Everything is buried in the snow. We'll have to take our chances."

For a while they walked in silence, crunching the frozen layer just below the fresh, soft powder underneath their feet. The snow-tipped branches of the trees on both sides of the curving path were glittering; the ground beneath them glittered too. Gad trained Hannah's flashlight well ahead of them, so that a little ball of light swung like a pendulum high on the dark trunks of distant trees.

Did the studios all really have fireplaces? Hannah wanted to know. Gad thought so, yes. Then would he teach her how to light a fire? She dropped her voice to a whisper, confessing: I've never even been up close to a fireplace. I've hardly ever even been in the same room with one. And there's one in my bedroom too; it's terribly intimidating.

Gad—who'd never imagined there might come a
moment in his life when he would be the expert in such matters—said that naturally he'd teach her; it was easy and he
thought she'd find it pleasant, as he did, to start the work day
with this ritual. He saw no reason to mention that he had just
learned himself, through trial and error (a great many errors)
how to light a fire; or that although he had lived once, for several years while Janet was in graduate school, in a rented house
that had a fireplace, he had never built a fire in it—that
was Janet's job, for she had grown up in Connecticut in a big
country house that had not one but two stone fireplaces; or
that, when they'd moved again, when it was Gad's turn to
start school while Janet finished up her dissertation, and they
were once more living in a proper tenement, only Janet
mourned the fireplace: Gad had said a silent prayer of thanks
that he would never have to feel a failure before a damned
hearth again.

Had Janet been here with him now—and what a
thought *that* was—she would have insisted on his saying all of
this. She would have refused to let him "get away" with pos-
ing as someone who knew how to build fires. Who *liked* building fires. Who was not afraid to walk into the woods at night.
"O, brave Indian guide!" she would have said. "Lead us not
into temptation!" That was just the sort of thing she thought
was funny. She would have mocked him for the way he held
the flashlight—she would have mocked him just for taking
charge of the flashlight. "What's next?" he could hear her saying. "Plotting a course by the stars?"

Was it any wonder, he asked himself, that he hadn't
called her? That he hadn't wanted to have to tell her anything
about what these last two weeks had been like for him? He
knew what she would have said: "Poor little matchboy." If he
had expected sympathy, empathy—even a few seconds' worth
of fellow-feeling, of even perfunctory commiseration—he
would have been barking up the wrong species of tree entirely.

And while she wouldn't have come out and said, "You see? That's what you get for not taking my advice," she would have made sure to imply exactly that in everything she did say. She would have done her best to leave him feeling worse than he'd been feeling on his own. Her *advice!* he thought, in a fury that had come upon him so suddenly he stopped where he was. Was it any wonder that he hadn't taken any of his wife's advice on how to keep from being disliked, when though she did not admit it—and perhaps did not quite know it—she disliked him too?

Hannah had kept on along the path. The flashlight made a broad pale circle on the ground ahead of her and she walked into it without having noticed that he wasn't going anywhere. Her black curls swung and bounced behind her, the tasseled end of her long childish hat bobbing among them. Her hair, he saw now, was longer than it had seemed to be on first glance: a tug on a ringlet, he thought, would double, maybe triple its length. This too made him think of Janet—made him think of the day, years ago, when she'd cut off all her hair without having told him that she meant to. She'd rung the doorbell, as a joke, when she'd come home after the haircut, and then she had been angry with *him*, both because he hadn't recognized her right away (although it had been only a matter of half-seconds before he had—really just the briefest hesitation) and because he hadn't told her that he liked it and that she looked beautiful. He *didn't* like it; she didn't look beautiful. Even now, even after all this time, he hadn't grown accustomed to it, nor had he come to like it. And he felt sure that despite Janet's insistence that she'd kept it so short all these years just because it was much easier to care for than it had been when she'd worn it long (for him, she said: *she'd* never really liked it) and saved her time she couldn't spare—a claim he doubted, since she seemed always to be running to the hairdresser's (which doubled as an art gallery, and boasted an espresso maker and a stack of copies of *Art Forum* along with the fanned

out *Vogue*s and *Cosmopolitan*s) to have it cut and "shaped," and
spent so many hours there each time she went—the real reason, the obvious and only reason she would not let it grow
out, was to spite him. Because she knew—he'd never hidden—
how he felt about it.

He hurried to catch up with Hannah.

Later he could not recall what they had talked about
on the rest of their walk through the woods, or afterwards,
in her studio. He remembered that he had admired the studio, and that he had, as promised, taught her how to build
and light a fire; also that at her request he'd tried the piano
and found that it had been tuned, and promised to play
something "all the way through" for her some other time—
but after he had said that, as they sat together by the fire,
what had they said? And when the fire died out, and they
walked back? He tried, as he lay in his bed, in the newest
and flimsiest of the sleeping dorms, to reconstruct their conversation, and his frustration—his inability to recall a single
specific thing that either of them had said—kept him awake
until it grew so late he became anxious about *that*, for if
he didn't get a good night's sleep how would he work
tomorrow? Such worry made it impossible to fall asleep.
He stole glances at his watch, which glowed on the
nightstand, and became more and more anxious. It was a
terrible night.

Hannah was already in the dining room when he
dragged himself in, exhausted, the next morning—he had slept
perhaps three hours, all told—and there was no place available beside her. He nodded morosely as he walked by the
table where she sat chatting with Keech and Azzoli and some
of the others. But after he had fetched his cereal and coffee,
and in the foulest of moods sat down at the only empty table,
his back to her, she suddenly appeared beside him, her own
bowl and cup in hand, the semi-precious stones glinting about
them like colored stars. "May I?" she said.

He made an effort not to look too pleased—it would be embarrassing—but his gloom lifted so swiftly (a black cloud rising and then in the air above him vanishing abruptly, like steam—but steam in a cartoon, not life: he imagined he could hear it hiss, then pop) he laughed out loud once, a bark that Hannah responded to with a soft laugh of her own.

"Good morning," he said as she sat down next to him. He was filled with happiness; it shocked him. "Sleep well?"

"I never do." She shrugged. "You?"

"Almost always. Not last night, though." He quickly added, "I can't imagine why. Just bad luck, I guess."

"I was born with it—insomnia, I mean, not bad luck. Though maybe that too." Before Gad could reply to this—he meant to protest—she said, "It's okay. They tell me I didn't sleep much even as a baby—my mother's bad luck, she says. Anyway, I'm used to it. If you're not, I bet it's really awful. You must be exhausted."

Gad nodded. But in fact, he realized then, he wasn't anymore. His tiredness had fled along with his ill humor.

"Will you be able to work?" she asked him.

He was so moved by her concern, by the kind—even tender—way she'd asked the question, tears sprang to his eyes. *Oh, for godsakes*, he thought. *Don't*. He bowed his head and scooped up a large spoonful of oatmeal. And then, immediately, another. Only when he was quite sure that he could speak without shaking loose any tears did he stop shoveling cereal into his mouth and say, "Oh, well—yes, probably." *Idiot*, he thought.

"Good," Hannah said, and she leaned in closer, lowering her voice as she began to tell him about the conversation she had just excused herself from at the other table. Keech had made certain she knew that he had solo shows in Rome and in L.A. next year. Azzoli, she reported, had told her the story of how he had once persuaded all the occupants of a skyscraper in lower Manhattan to turn their lights on and off at prescribed intervals, and how he'd photographed the "gor-geous" results. "Available for viewing in his studio."

"No etchings?" Gad said.

"No. Ken Adams has the etchings—seriously." And she told him that she really had been asked if she would like to "drop in anytime" to see some etchings by the printmaker from Iowa with whom Gad had never exchanged a word; he hadn't even known his name until Hannah told him. Also— Hannah was giggling now—a writer who had sat with them last night, whose name was something like Ben Benson or John Johnson or Nick Nixon (by the time the introductions had come round to him, Gad had not only ceased to take stabs at names, he had stopped listening, and Hannah referred to him now as the I'm-Less-Famous-Than-I-Should-Be-And-I'll-Tell-You-Why Short Story Writer), had made it his business to let Hannah know that he'd had stories in four out of the last six annual *Best American Short Stories*, won three O'Henry's, and had a story coming out in next month's *Harper's*. "And two of the people I was sitting with have won the Rome Prize," Hannah told Gad, who said, "What, no Nobel Prizes? You must have been slumming."

There had been only one person at the table, besides her, said Hannah, who'd never been here or to any other art-ists' colony before. "And she says she's the only female sculp-tor in residence here, and one of only three female visual art-ists who've been here all month." "Oh, yes." Gad sighed. He knew her. She worked "in miniature," on the floor of her stu-dio. She made small, fragile piles of things, and when she'd held her open studio, Gad had accidentally stepped on a four-inch high sloping tower made of squares of colored wax, and then, trying to right himself, slid first on a pile of stones beside it and then into a tiny mountain made of broken glass. Her first name, he had no trouble recalling, was Mad, short for Madeline. "Mad Eastwood," he said.

"Close. Mad Westfield." Hannah grinned.

"Right. So what did you say to them?"

"Me? I told them all about my cat." Her eyes gleamed with mischief. For the first time he noticed their color—the precise color of the stone on the ring she wore on her right index finger: the blue-gray of the Atlantic Ocean once you got out where you could no longer stand. He'd never met anyone with gray eyes before; he'd always assumed that calling someone's eyes "gray" was a literary conceit. "They seemed very interested," Hannah said.

"Did they?" he asked. "What exactly did you tell them?"

Hannah dipped her spoon into her bowl but only stirred; she didn't lift it out again. "Oh, I told them the story of her life. As much of it as I know, anyway. Starting with how I found her in a snowdrift near Sheridan Square. At midnight." She let her spoon fall against the side of her bowl. "Soggy," she said. "I hate soggy corn flakes."

"Why don't you get some oatmeal? Or eggs? They'll make you eggs if you ask."

"I hate breakfast, actually." She pushed her bowl away from her, toward the center of the table. "It's a heartwarming story, really. And dramatic, too, in its way. Not much happens, of course, but there's plenty of emotion. Ups and downs."

"I see," Gad said. "And they listened?"

"I don't think they listened," she said soberly.

He laughed. "You're a funny girl."

"Oh, I know it," she said.

They walked outside together. On the porch he offered to walk her to her studio, but she said that she thought she'd like to try to find it on her own. He swallowed his disappointment, told himself that it was foolish of him to mind: he'd get to his own studio, and down to work, that much sooner this way. "I'll see you at dinner, then," he said casually. Hannah said, "Yes, I'll save you a place if I get there first. You do the same, all right?" And as she stood looking up at him he was once more confused by what was stirred up in him—pleasure and unease, both; a flickering sort of thrill, along with dismay; comfort and discomfort in what seemed equal parts—and he remembered suddenly how puzzled he had been when he had first met Janet, how, as he'd stood gazing up at *her* (*way* up, it had seemed to him, for she was perched atop those strapped-on blocks of cork that girls were wearing then as shoes—although it wasn't until later on that night, after she'd kicked them off in his dorm room, that he became aware of that, and even that confused him, as it disappointed *and* relieved him to discover that she wasn't as much taller than he was as he had first believed) he couldn't make up his mind how he felt. He hadn't thought of this in years—had actively suppressed it, he thought, almost as it was occurring. What he had told himself about that night was that while he hadn't been *attracted* to her size, exactly, it had been compelling to him: it had drawn him in, drawn him toward her. That was a kind of attraction, he allowed, but a kind that had nothing to do with allure, with temptation. The story he told himself (and years later told the women who required explanation) was all about how reassuring, how *essential*, Janet's size had been to the unconfident, self-conscious boy "sorely in need of shelter" he had been; it was about how sturdy and substantial she had seemed to him then.

But he remembered now (remembered not just standing with her in a corner at the dance where they had met, talking intently for so many hours, until they were shooed from the room that had already emptied, but also later, in his room, the tangled-up mound of her clothes and his on the orange carpet by his bed) the clash of feelings in him. He'd been compelled toward her, that much was true; but he had been repelled as well. And he didn't trust himself—his own yearning or his lust. He remembered that. She seemed substantial, all right. Even in bed, naked, she was strong and solid. She had the broad back and shoulders of the swimmer she had once been (or so she said—he had to take her word for it, for she had ceased to swim before they'd met: a crisis, she said, as she'd hoped for the Olympics—and to this day she'd never told him why she'd stopped). He was impressed with her, but also worried and uneasy, even as they rolled together in the circumscribed space of the narrow bed—pawing at each other as silently as possible, so as not to disturb the roommate sleeping, or pretending to sleep, across the room from them (the roommate who requested to be moved soon after, and whose name Gad had forgotten; Janet, for her part, had always claimed not to recall he'd ever *had* a roommate). He worried that she might be "too much for him" (how much space she took up in the little bed! How strange it was to hold in his arms someone whose back and long-muscled arms felt stronger than his own; whose legs were longer, shoulders wider; whose strong hands pressed on his back were—he had already discovered as they'd walked the long way across campus, fingers entwined and hips bumping, to his room—larger than his) and he worried that there might be something suspect in his very interest in her.

Hannah was looking at him quizzically. He turned away, shading his eyes as if the sun were troubling him. "Good luck today," he said. "First day might be tough. But"—he coughed out something like a laugh—"maybe not. I don't know. New surroundings. Bit of a shock, maybe. Though that did me good, I think. Anyway"—he started down the steps without looking at her—"break a leg, you know, and all that."

It was possible that she said something in response—he thought he might have heard her say something—but he was down the steps by then and halfway to the path that led him to his studio, and he just kept going.

His day went exactly as he'd feared it would. His concentration was terrible; he felt slow and stupid, too tired to think clearly and at the same time agitated, too wound up to nap or even rest, although he made himself lie down, not just

after lunch as always, but three other times, for fifteen minutes each. But lying still, his arms pressed to his sides, his eyes
closed, *trying* to sleep, made him jumpier. He thought of
Hannah in *her* studio: saw her sitting first at the long desk under the window with a typewriter before her and a sheet of
yellow paper in it, half-filled up with type (ah, now—finally—
there was something he remembered that they'd spoken of last
night: her typewriter and her reams of yellow paper. *Habit*,
she had said, and laughed, *or superstition. I wrote my first poems, when I was six years old, on a cast-off Smith Corona manual
my father gave me, on the yellow newsprint he brought home from
work*), then in the padded rocker with a notebook open on her
lap (. . .*but I begin most things in a notebook. I just make lines—
images, ideas—until something starts to come from them. It's sort
of random at that point, though really the idea of "automatic writing" makes me a little queasy. It sounds like playing with a Ouija
board, doesn't it?*), then on a cushion by the fireplace (thinking,
resting, staring at the fire she'd made with his instructions fresh
in her mind—hearing his voice in her mind as she laid kindling)—saw her here and there amid the things she had been
so delighted by last night. Saw her working, happily, and saw
stacks of typed-on yellow paper piling up on every surface.

He groaned. The Hollywood movie version of a
writer's day. The *cartoon* version. Bugs Bunny as a poet. The
poems would pile up, fill the cabin, burst its seams, and *boom!*—
wooden shingles, windows, furniture, and millions of poems
typed on yellow paper would explode in all directions.

He was ashamed of himself. Both for the banality of
his imagination and for what the images he'd summoned up
suggested. Was he jealous? Angry that she might be having a
good day—a perfect day—while he was in here struggling?
Was he *blaming* her?

He wasn't blaming anyone, he told himself. Not even
himself. He was tired, that was all, and being tired led to being easily distracted. By now he'd given up on working and

was doing busywork instead—straightening up and filing away the notes he'd made since coming here, glancing at the "professional" mail that he'd arranged to have reach him at the Colony (the only mail, he had warned Janet, that he'd wished to have sent here) and answering some of it—filling up the time remaining and reminding himself that along with being tired, which was bad enough, the trouble was that his plan for today had been to start on the concerto, and that starting something new was always difficult. "Difficult" was in fact putting it mildly. Starting something new was terrible— so much harder than continuing something that he often fantasized a lifelong work in progress. A *Remembrance of Things Past.* Ever since Janet had mentioned, two or three years ago, that Proust had still been working on the endless multi-volume novel at his death (she was rereading parts of it for a seminar that she was teaching on "Privileging Memory in Proust, Joyce, Bellow, and Brodkey"), he had entertained, almost but not quite seriously, this idea. What a relief it would be to never have to begin again!

That this concerto had actually been commissioned— that there was an up-and-coming, if small (if obscure, he told himself; if mediocre; if—*for pity's sake*, he thought, in a sudden-blooming rage of pure self-loathing—*if Midwestern*) orchestra waiting for it—was all the extra pressure that he needed to make it impossible for him to do anything today.

At last he gave up even on busywork. He left the studio, went to his bedroom and did nothing—sat on the bed and stared at the wall until the remaining hour and a half before dinner had passed, promising himself without conviction that the next day would be better, that a good night's sleep and the mental trick of persuading himself that tomorrow was the second, not the first, day of his work on the concerto that he had been asked to write for the small, perfectly respectable Middle Western orchestra (which, he had to remind himself, he had been thrilled about; he had

been overjoyed, and wildly flattered, he thought dolefully)
would fix the problem.

Which—remarkably—it seemed to do. The next day,
perhaps fueled in part by an exchange with Hannah during
dinner about her "glorious" first day ("I broke a leg, I did!"
she'd called to him from far across the dining room when he'd
come in, and everyone looked up, then down again immediately—because it was only he who'd come into the room? Or
because they disapproved of her? She *was* like a child among
them, he thought as he hurried over; just then, he was embarrassed for her. But as he sat down in the chair she'd saved for
him, and she reached for his hand and squeezed it, saying,
"This is heaven. It's perfection. I refuse to ever leave," he
found himself so touched by her fervency, so grateful for her
very artlessness, that his despondency was vanquished. Indeed, he cheered up so thoroughly and so abruptly that he
laughed; then Hannah started laughing too, and he felt purely
joyful), fortified by nine hours of sleep and an embryonic idea
for the new piece that had just begun to form as he woke up
that morning, he worked soundly, solidly, and swiftly. And
by the next day, the first movement of the concerto firmly underway, the hours flew by so quickly—he ate lunch at the piano and then skipped his nap, reluctant to stop working—and
every thought came so clearly and easily, he decided that his
one bad day was anomalous: it was as if it never had occurred
at all.

His work went so well now, day after day—even better, he marveled, than before Hannah's arrival—that he began
to think of her, he told her at breakfast at the start of her sixth
day, as his inspiration. He said it as if he were joking, which
he wasn't. The truth was that the thought of her, joyfully at
work in her own cabin at the far end of the Colony, slipped in
and out of his mind all day long and urged him on—*cheered*
him on. He imagined her and he felt happy—it seemed quite
that simple. "You're a veritable one-girl booster squad," he

told her, and he laughed; if she laughed too, then it would be a joke between them.

But she didn't. "I'm glad," she said. "It's only fair. Because when *I'm* stuck, when I've been staring at a line for twenty minutes and I know there's something wrong but I can't fix it, when I find myself thinking again and again of the same three or four unacceptable solutions to the problem, I give myself a spectral break: I take a nice long walk over to your place and I let myself in and just stand there behind you watching until my mind unfreezes."

Gad blushed. "And this does the trick?"

"Oh, yes. Ten minutes or so and I'm back to work, knowing exactly what to do."

"Ten minutes," murmured Gad. "And I never even offer you a cup of tea? How very rude." Now Hannah laughed. "So. . ." Gad said. "How do things sound over there, then?"

"Inspired," said Hannah seriously, and Gad blushed again.

His days were sweetened, brightened, by her—and not only by the thought of her at work, or by the new thought she had inserted into his mind (for he found himself now at various times throughout the day imagining her imagining him, which was unnerving in the most pleasant way), but by his very gladness for and utter lack of envy of her when she told him how well her own work was going. That he could be so munificent was a revelation to him.

He confessed this to her—he was compelled, it seemed, to make a full confession to her of every passing thought—as they took their long after-dinner walk one night. "Silly," she said, punching his shoulder with her mittened fist. "Silly of you not to have already known how generous your spirit is."

They had by this time established the habit of these nightly walks. He held her flashlight. When the path was slippery he took her arm. Sometimes they wandered up and down the paths that curled through the woods and snaked around the studios for two hours or more before they said goodnight. If there was a reading or a slide show or an open studio, they walked for an hour before it started and then for another hour right afterwards; they'd begin the second hour talking about what they'd heard or seen, and these performances—which he had endured stoically before Hannah's arrival—seemed much more interesting to him once they became the jumping-off points for his and Hannah's conversations. It never took long for an assessment of someone's most recent efforts—novels in progress about sad, squabbling families or adolescent rites of passage; short stories about hostile marriages; poetry describing in excruciating detail childhood memories or the poet's elegantly multilayered response to a painting or a piece of music; paintings and sculpture that could not be said to be "about" anything at all except (so one of the painters had announced) "the praxis of art-making itself"—to lead them back to their ongoing subject: themselves and each other.

Indeed, by the time the second week of Hannah's residency was well underway, they had ceased to attend these presentations; they'd made a pact, too, not to give their own. "They're a little bit embarrassing, don't you think?" Hannah said. "They're too much like 'show and tell.'" Gad could not have been more pleased, but to make sure that she was not capitulating to his own unspoken wishes, he said, "But you know they say it's part of the experience of being here. I don't want you to feel that you've missed out on anything."

"Oh," Hannah said airily, "I don't think I'll be missing anything. I've got the picture by now pretty well."

Still, once—hearing laughter in the distance as they walked—Gad felt a spark of guilt that flared and died so quickly he had to guess at its meaning. Hannah was talking just then about a novel she'd begun to read the night before (she was, despite her voiced disdain for the Colony's performances of works in progress, a great one for new novels and

new books of poems and stories—she was providing him with
the education Janet had always been irritated with him for not
wanting). When she paused, before she could go on to offer
up an anecdote about her life, of which she'd been reminded
by something she'd just said about the novel, or ask him one
of her odd questions (What were you like in elementary school?
What kinds of places did you go on dates in high school?
What's your favorite movie—novel/painting/piece of music/
pop song/rock band/board game—of all time? Which did
you identify with: the tin man, the scarecrow, the cowardly
lion, or Dorothy?), he asked her if she didn't mind that he had
been monopolizing all of her attention and her time whenever
she was not at work. Perhaps she'd like to get to know the
others while she had the chance?

"To get to know the others?" Gad thought for that
instant that she sounded truly puzzled. Then she giggled. "Oh,
but I know them so *well*. I know what they do and where
they live and *how* they live and where they're from originally—
not to mention where they went to school and where they
didn't go to school, and why—and what they've all been working on for the past year and what they're going to do next.
And furthermore"—she paused dramatically—"*I* know all
their names."

In fact by then she didn't, but Gad didn't point this
out. He saw no reason to mention that since she'd arrived
new people had come and old ones had gone, and that she
hadn't exchanged so much as a word with anyone since her
first morning here. She'd made her point, he decided. He felt
absolved. Let the others sit in a hushed circle while someone
showed slides of mixed-media paintings "blending banal contemporary domestic materials with body-related issues and
references to iconic works of art of the nineteenth century."
Let them afterwards go off in groups of eight or ten, stum-
bling drunk, to contemplate the moon. He and Hannah would
continue to hurry through their dinner (the food wasn't very

good anyway, and the room was noisy; it was impossible to have a private conversation), then slip out to take their walk and tell each other stories and swap such news as there was about their workdays.

He was about to tell her about the deer that had come right up to his window today and stood there for a long time—listening, he had to believe, for the deer didn't leave until he stopped playing, at which point it suddenly bolted—when she said, "Speaking of names ...."

He groaned, as he was expected to, for this had become part of their routine too. Every night, at some point during their walk, she would report that she had yet to "uncover"—the verb was hers—the perfect name for him; he was to remain nameless for another day.

But she said, "I've made a decision," and Gad was taken entirely by surprise by how fearful and anxious this announcement made him. It was as if he thought she really must have uncovered something, some terrible secret about him, after all these days of pondering.

"I've decided you don't need a name, after all." She said this gravely, and it shocked him that he felt so wounded.

He tried for a light tone as he said, "So I'm to remain 'covered' forever, then? Does this conclusion mean that you've given up because I am so thoroughly impenetrable, or that so many interesting possibilities suggested themselves you simply couldn't choose one, for fear that it would be reductive? Or have you decided that unlike other mortals I simply don't require designation?"

"Don't read so much into it," Hannah said.

"Well, what if we were separated in the woods"—he couldn't help it, somehow; he couldn't make himself stop, though he felt foolish—"how would you call out to me?"

"Why would we be separated?"

"If we were," he insisted.

"In that case I suppose I would have to rely on the

designation I use when I refer to you in my journal"—and at once Gad's heart lifted in relief (she *referred* to him: she wrote about him; therefore, his insignificance could not be the explanation for her decision)—"which is simply 'G.' So that if for some inexplicable reason we became separated in the woods, I could call, 'G!' and you would know that it was you I was searching for."

"Gee," he said lamely.

"Exactly," Hannah said.

That next afternoon they took a midday break together—he forfeited his post-lunch nap—and went into town. They bought two bottles of wine, having decided during last night's walk that it would be pleasant to have a glass of wine apiece with dinner, and then Hannah helped him choose a tall pair of thick rubber boots. This was her idea. She had been fretting, she said, over his bootless treks through the snow. And yesterday the temperature had begun to nudge upward: the snow was melting. Any day now, Hannah pointed out, the Colony would be awash in mud.

Indeed, spring—such as it was, at the Colony—had come. Within a few days, as the temperature inched up and the sun shone all day long, the snow melted into narrow rivers that crisscrossed the Colony; always now there was the sound of rushing water. Gad sat in his studio and listened. He opened his windows for the first time since his arrival, and in came the gurgling, the water-clatter; also the metronomic drip of water off the cabin's roof. He heard too for the first time all the sounds of small animals and birds hidden in the woods around him.

And outside, everywhere, there was mud—the deepest, thickest mud imaginable. He'd never seen anything remotely like it. As Hannah looked on, laughing, he bent down and, balancing on the soles of his new boots, he plunged one bare hand as deeply into it as he could. The mud was ice-cold—for a second he thought his heart might stop—and when he pulled his hand out, clumps of it clung resolutely to his skin. His coat sleeve was coated with mud too—two or three inches up, as if it had been dipped in pudding. It would never come out. As he considered this (how unlike him it was to have done this!), he laughed in a way that seemed peculiar even to him. Laughed, and felt his eyes film over: tears.

Mud, and slim muddy rivers racing one another—that was the terrain now. It looked impassable; it would have been, in his old hiking boots. But in the rubber boots that Hannah had picked out for him—tall, dark green and shiny, like a pair he thought he could remember having had when he was nine or ten years old—he was able to tramp through it easily. The sucking sound the boots made with each step pleased him, the way it would have pleased him at age nine.

Hannah had retired her puffy jacket and switched to a thick, stiff-looking sweater that zipped up. Lime green with little flecks of brown and white. She'd exchanged the stocking cap for a brown felt beret. Gad celebrated spring by wearing his black coat unbuttoned. They had noticed that the mound of jackets, coats, gloves, sweaters, down-filled vests, wool hats and scarves piled high in the corner of the Commons Room each morning and evening during meals was shrinking daily. (Gad had told Hannah, early on, that this was a twice-daily "instant installation"; he'd sworn that during both breakfast and dinner one of the conceptual artists would sneak out and photograph it, so that when his residency ended he'd have documentation of the eighty-four installations he'd participated in during his stay at the Colony. Hannah now said, straight-faced, that the fellow might have trouble filling all four walls of a gallery for his next show. "Unless—here's an idea—the last ten or twelve shots are of an empty corner." "Ah, yes," Gad said. "Very moving.")

Two weeks had passed now since Hannah's first day at the Colony. The days—abruptly, it seemed—became noticeably longer. It was still light out now when they finished dinner and began their walks, so that if Gad said something that made Hannah laugh, he could watch her, not just listen. He told her what her laugh "did"—dimmed the houselights, lit the stage.

"Is that so?" Hannah said, and laughed some more. "What's on stage, then?" Fully lit, beringed hands on hips— or what he imagined were her hips, hidden beneath the long, stiff lime green sweater.

"Your true loveliness," he said. "In its every aspect."

She smacked his arm. "You're awfully corny, you know that? But also, I must say"— she linked her arm through the one she'd struck—"very sweet. Really." He knew she meant that she thought he was lying, or at the very least exaggerating. She was "no beauty," she knew—so she had once told him, so casually that he understood this to be her sincere opinion of herself.

They had by now confessed to each other many such privately held convictions. They had each handed over, Gad joked, an annotated "lifetime personal report card," using the grading system of the New York City public elementary schools of both of their childhoods—excellent, good, fair, and unsatisfactory (it was in this context that Gad remembered, and told Hannah, what he had not thought about in decades: that he had been judged "unsatisfactory" in "shows self-control," and "fair" in every other category of "personal and social development and behavior" on every single one of his thrice-yearly report cards through sixth grade, to his mother's tearful, hand-wringing dismay)—and they had come to understand each other, Gad believed, as deeply as if they had known each other for years rather than weeks.

And why not, when all they did all day was work in their studios and talk to each other? There *was* nothing else. Each of them made certain gestures toward life outside, beyond the Colony's stone walls—Gad sent two picture postcards of the Colony to Janet (the first one, finally, after he re-

ceived a brief, chiding note from her) and Hannah called Saint
John once ("He understands that I'm not going to be in constant touch. He knows what I'm here for," she told Gad);
Hannah typed a letter for Gad, from his scrawled draft, to
the director of the orchestra that had commissioned the concerto, telling him (at Hannah's urging) that he was ahead of
schedule; Hannah made notes in the margins of a fat anthol-
ogy of poems in preparation for a course she had been asked
to teach at the Y in the summer—but "real life," they agreed,
seemed by and large so nebulous and distant it was as if
they had dreamed, not lived it. Indeed, Hannah remarked,
sometimes when they talked about their lives she had the feeling that they were exchanging dreams instead of factual ac-
counts—for they both told their stories with that urgency, that
inexplicable intensity that she associated with the telling of a
dream the morning after. Hushed and mystified and yet insistent. And so many of the details, even to the teller, seemed
absurd—unthinkable.

By this time they had exhausted the stories of their
early lives. They knew each other's childhoods practically by
heart—they gave pop quizzes to each other, teasing: "My best
friend from age four till thirteen?" (Hannah's prompt to Gad,
who'd sigh and say, "Oh, please, why don't you ask me something *hard*? That's one Miss Josephine Versace, of the yard-
long braids and cold spaghetti sandwiches on hero bread for
lunch, the homemade jumpers and embroidered blouses that
you coveted, and the uncanny gift for drawing any kind of
animal")—and they had a pretty good feel for the recent past;
they were nearly up to date. Hannah had already told him
how she'd met "the saint"—so Gad had come to think of him—
and how their romance had started. They'd met, "strangely
enough," she'd told him, at a poker game. In Hell's Kitchen.
"Definitely not his usual milieu. So it must have been fate."

"But a poker game is *your* milieu? You're a gambler?"

"Not is but was. And only glancingly." And in response to his raised eyebrow: "A nickel-dime game, okay? A quarter limit, three raises tops. I'm no gambler—never have been. A photographer I used to know had a Friday night game that people were always dropping in and out of. Mostly actors and playwrights, mostly from the neighborhood. Jack— that's the photographer—used to go out with my next-door neighbor. A rock musician, a guitarist. She hated poker. And she was always working on Friday nights. Anyway, I played occasionally. And one night Saint John turned up, the guest of an actor who lived next door to *him*, downtown. He told us he thought John could use a night out, and a chance to meet some artists. 'He has a very boring life'—that's actually how he introduced him to the rest of us."

"And you fell in love with him?"

"I felt sorry for him. Love came later."

On another night, she'd told Gad how they'd started "keeping company"—a phrase that Gad found charming— soon after that first meeting. She had been surprised when he'd called her, surprised that he'd gone to the trouble to track down her phone number.

"Industrious," Gad had commented.

"Yes," Hannah had said. "Exactly."

She'd told Gad all about their "weird dates": an afternoon at the transit museum in Brooklyn, with the ten-year-old boy he was a Big Brother to in tow; a lecture on "the new Cuba" at the Little Red Schoolhouse; a meeting of the Coalition to Save Alphabet City, and one for AIDS volunteers.

Tonight he thought to ask her how long ago all of this had happened.

"Oh, long," Hannah said. "The same year I finished school."

"And how long have you been. . .you're engaged, right?"

"Also long." She laughed. "Very, very long." Then she turned serious. He heard it even before she spoke again, in the way she paused and took an odd, short breath—and he felt it in the way she tightened her hold on his arm as they walked. And when she spoke, after a little while, her intonation was not merely serious but bleak. "So how did you and Janet decide to get married, anyway?"

"I'm not sure we ever did. Decide to, I mean. I'm pretty sure we did get married." But Hannah didn't laugh. Lightly, Gad said, "For us it was more along the lines of, 'well, now it's time to do this' than it was an actual decision anybody made."

Hannah sighed so deeply, so feelingly, Gad was reminded of the line in the old song—"With love to lead the way/ I've found more clouds of gray/ than any Russian play/could guarantee"—but he thought better of singing it aloud. "The thing is," she was saying, "Saint John and I do nothing but *try* to decide. We just can't seem to. We can't even decide to live together. Or *where* we'd live. Or, when we do get married, how and where we'll do it. He's ten years older than I am— just your age, I guess,"—and she said this as if it were a surprise to her—"and he says that's partly why it's so hard for us to make a decision together. The difference in our ages, plus the difference in our temperaments, provides each of us with a different decision-making style."

"His phrasing, I assume?" Gad said dryly, but Hannah nodded without having noticed *how* he'd said it.

"That, plus his being so cautious by nature—he has to consider every angle, every detail, over and over again—and my being so indecisive—I guess by nature too—leaves us in limbo. We've been planning to get married for four—no," she corrected herself, "it's closer to five years now. And *planning* is a gross overstatement. Talking about it. Saying we will. Just not ever doing anything about it."

"Janet and I never planned it. We just did it. We felt— *I* felt, I guess I should say—I can't speak for her, naturally. I don't know how she felt. I felt we had to."

"Had to," Hannah murmured. And then, switching to the tone that she reserved for quoting lines from poetry (delicately theatrical; faintly ironic—by now he could identify it from the first word uttered in this vein), complete with the just barely perceptible pauses that indicated where a line broke on the page, she said: "'To have to/is an odd infinitive, in which/compulsion and possession meet/and share a word together.'"

Gad kept silent. This was something else he'd learned by now: that it was always best not to say anything when she recited poetry, especially since he could never tell what was her own and what was someone else's.

She sighed again. Then she laughed, but it was a gloomy-sounding affair. "You know, I've actually thought of that poem by Heather McHugh in terms of Saint John and me. It ends: 'It's odd because they're two at one/but endless, in the end, in their/capacity to be attached. . .' It actually ends with ellipses. Isn't that odd? As if you were to fill in the blank: 'their capacity to be attached'. . .to what?"

"I should think the 'blank' is meant to be filled in 'to each other,'" Gad said.

"Exactly my point," she said, as eagerly as if for the moment she imagined she were teaching a class. "You see, I don't know if it *can* be filled in that way."

Confused, Gad said, "So you don't think that you and Saint John are endless in your capacity to 'be attached'?"

"Oh, to be attached, yes. But to each other? I don't *know*."

She had said this so woefully—she sounded close to tears—that Gad, on impulse, unlinked his arm from hers and took her hand instead. He held it tightly as they walked on.

They'd both been silent for much longer than usual when he said, "Do you remember the story of how Janet and I met?"

"At a dance at Wesleyan. You talked for hours. She told you that she considered herself 'a woman who thinks,' and as soon as she said it you knew you'd ask her back to your room, because all the girls you'd met till then in college had disappointed you. You'd gone up there expecting 'thinkers'— smart girls with ideas who could keep up their end of an interesting conversation. You'd imagined yourself falling in love with such a girl. So it was as if she knew what you needed. She'd said the magic words."

Gad laughed; he gripped her hand even tighter. That version of the story, which he'd told her several nights ago, was as true as the one he usually told, the one that emphasized how sturdy and solid Janet had seemed when he had first met her. He had some doubts about that explanation now: was that really what had brought them together? At least what he'd told Hannah had the virtue of being literally true, based on a scrap of remembered conversation.

"Then she went back to your room with you," Hannah said. "You tried not to wake your roommate. In the morning he was furious and told you both off."

"Yes, he did."

"Then what happened?" Hannah asked, as if this were a fairy tale. As if she were a child and he were telling her a bedtime story.

"That's what I wanted to tell you." Still, he hesitated; he wasn't sure why. "She never left. That's how we started living together."

Hannah took this in. He was grateful that she didn't say, "You started living with her the first night you met!" or anything along those lines—anything that sounded critical or even surprised. For a moment she didn't speak at all, and then when she did she just said, "So when did you get married?"

"A little less than three years later. As soon as I graduated."

"From college?" Now she sounded surprised, even shocked. But he discovered that he didn't mind. "That young? Really?"

"I'm afraid so."

"But how could you have been sure enough of your-selves at that age?"

Somehow, her surprise—her disbelief—was endear-ing to him. "Well, we weren't, really," he said. "We thought we were, I guess, but we weren't." He didn't say, *She* thought we were, though that was closer to the truth. He had just gone along with what she'd thought, or at least what she'd said. He'd still been young enough to just do things without think-ing them through, without thinking about what the conse-quences might be. And Janet had seemed so sure of herself that it hadn't even crossed his mind to protest.

"Saint John talks about the 'history' he and I have to-gether," Hannah said. "As if that explains everything. As if that alone would justify our decision. Assuming we ever ac-tually make one. But 'history' isn't enough to keep you go-ing, is it?"

"I don't know," Gad admitted.

Janet had been two years ahead of him at school. When he graduated, she didn't have to remind him that she'd been marking time for the two years since her own graduation, waiting tables. Waiting for him. She was about to start gradu-ate school, finally; they'd never even talked about the possi-bility that he might not go with her. And Janet said it would be childish to travel together to a new town to set up house-keeping as "just boyfriend and girlfriend." So they moved as husband and wife.

He told this to Hannah. "And. . .?" she said.

"And what?"

"That doesn't seem like the end of the story."

"No? It's the end of every story I've ever heard. 'And so they married and lived happily ever after.'"

"Did you, then?"

"Did I what?" Though he knew what she meant.

"Did you and Janet live happily ever after?" When he

didn't answer, Hannah said, patiently, "I mean, do you still love each other? Are you happy together?"

"I'm not sure that's a question you ask yourself after you've been married as long as we have."

"Why not?"

"Because you just don't. Because that's not what's relevant."

"What's relevant," she echoed. He couldn't tell if she was mocking him or expressing wonder. "What *is*, then?"

"The stake you've taken in the marriage."

"Now you sound like Saint John. Your 'history,' you mean."

"No, I mean something more than that." He disliked being irritated with her; he tried to fight the feeling off.

"Something more like what?"

"Like once you've made the decision to spend your life with someone, that bears honoring."

"You never made a decision. You said so."

"I made the commitment. That's what counts."

"So it's a matter of not breaking promises?"

"Not just any promises. This is marriage we're talking about. The ties that bind, you know?"

"Bind as in 'make stick together'? Or as in 'obligate'? Or as in 'restrain'?"

"You're a walking thesaurus, aren't you," he said, more dourly than he would have expected.

"Sorry," Hannah said. And she sounded sorry, too; she wasn't just being polite. "I don't know why I'm giving you such a hard time."

"You're not." He made himself laugh. "Though you might consider going into Saint John's line of work. You give a hell of a cross-examination."

They had stopped walking—he wasn't sure when. They stood in the woods, her left hand within his right. "I'm really sorry," Hannah said. "Let's talk about something else."

"No," he said. "*I'm* sorry. I'm being a jerk. Come on." He tugged her forward, and as they continued hand in hand along the path they could have walked along blindfolded by now, he said, "In answer to your question? Whether Janet and I still love each other?" He paused. "I don't know. The truth is I have no idea whatsoever. I don't even know what the question means after so many years."

"I don't know what the question means, either," Hannah said, "even after far fewer years."

They fell into a gloomy silence for a moment. "'Tied and bound with the chain of our sins,'" he murmured. It was one of the last things Janet had said to him before they'd parted at the airport. It was his turn to sigh like a character in a Russian play. "Let's start back, okay?"

She nodded. For the first time, they walked back without talking.

But as she slipped into the chair beside his at breakfast the next morning, Hannah said—as if there hadn't been a ten-hour pause in their conversation—"So if you had it to do over, would you marry Janet?"

"That's a terrible question," he said. "I hate that kind of question."

"Really? I love that kind of question."

"What kind? One that courts regret?"

"Oh, no"—she seemed genuinely surprised—"I didn't mean 'do you regret having married her?' I just meant, if you met her now for the first time, instead of then, would you fall in love with her? Would you end up together anyway?"

He shrugged. "I would be a different person now if I hadn't spent the last two decades with Janet."

"How? How, exactly?" Hannah asked him, with the fervor of a ten-year-old girl trying to make sense of grown-up life.

"I don't know *exactly*, Hannah. I don't know anything *exactly*."

"Doesn't that bother you?" But before he could respond—he was too nonplused by the question to be able to
answer it quickly—she said, "I want to know everything *exactly*." She tossed her head and her hair brushed his shoulder.
Ten years old? he thought. No, eight. *Six*.

He picked up a ringlet. Tugged it gently. Unwound,
these ringlets of hers would reach well down her back, he
thought—and the image of her that came to him then, her hair
uncurled (wet, as it would have to be, straight, black, and shin-
ing, draped around her back and shoulders) made him blush
and turn away.

"Good luck," he said, and Hannah laughed.

In his studio, after breakfast, he put twice as many logs
as usual in the fireplace grate, and more kindling than was
strictly necessary. A fire itself was probably unnecessary by
now, he reflected. But he didn't care. The fitful crackling of
the fire, as he turned his back to it, made him think of the uncertain, scattered bursts of quickly silenced applause between
movements that one always heard at concerts in the city where
he lived.

At dinner that night Hannah told him that she'd spent
the day on a new poem, a love poem. "A memory of love poem,"
she corrected herself. She told him that somehow she'd found
herself thinking today about the first time she'd imagined that
she was in love. She was in the third grade. She'd had two
crushes even before that, neither of which had lasted more than
a few days, but this feeling had not only lasted for a long time,
she had known immediately that it was more significant. "It
felt important," she said. "It felt like life and death."

"How is it that this stone has remained unturned until now?" Gad asked. He was bizarrely hurt, he realized. As if
she had been keeping a secret from him for years—like the
wife in that James Joyce story that ends with the husband
watching the snow. Janet had written a paper—in grad school?
in college?—on the image of snow in that story and some oth-

ers. He used to read all of her papers. He couldn't recall if he
had ever actually read the story.

"Buried," Hannah said, and he was startled. He must
have read the story: he could almost visualize the words on
the page. The cemetery. The grave of the wife's dead lover. "I
think it's one of those things that's so humiliating you just make
yourself stop thinking of it. I hadn't thought about it in years.
I would have sworn I'd forgotten."

"What was humiliating about it?"

"Oh, I so adored him! And I never told him. I could
hardly bring myself to speak to him at all."

So what ever became of him? Gad wanted to know.
But Hannah said she didn't have a clue. "His family moved
away when we were in the fifth grade and I never heard anything about him after that."

"You adored him in secret for two years?" They'd
left the dining room; they were walking now.

"For two years? I was in *high school* before I stopped
thinking about him. It didn't seem to make any difference that
he wasn't around."

"That's true devotion, all right. You were very steadfast."

"It's more like true idiocy," Hannah said. "I was stupid and stubborn. It was ridiculous. He never even knew
how I felt."

"What about him?"

"What *about* him?"

"How did he feel about you?"

"How would I know?" Hannah said. "I think I man-
aged to get up the nerve to speak to him twice. I once said,
'Mrs. Hochberg is really nice, isn't she?' and he said, 'Yeah.
She always writes, 'Very imaginative' on my book reports. Mrs.
Greenfield would just put a checkmark.'"

"You remember that?"

Hannah blushed. He'd never seen her blush before.
"It was *something*. That was the way I saw it, so I tucked it

away in my memory. And he *was* 'very imaginative.' He was smart and he wrote poetry, just like I did, and he could play the piano and sing, too. Mrs. Hochberg gave him the lead in our class play that year, and then he had the lead again in the fourth grade and he would have had it in the fifth grade too if he hadn't moved to Teaneck. Actually"—Hannah squinted up at him—"I bet he was a lot like you were at that age."

"I'm flattered," Gad said. And he was. "I didn't write poetry, though, and my book reports were never any good. But I would have been just as dense as he was, where you were concerned. I was pretty dense." And he was moved to tell her then about *his* first grade-school love—a story he'd forgotten to tell, even if he had not, as Hannah had, imagined that he had forgotten the object of his ardor. "I confessed my love to Roberta Shamah—I believe we were in fifth grade at the time—and she said, 'Don't be silly. I'm too popular to be *your* girlfriend.' I hadn't known that. Talk about humiliation! I wasn't in her league, she made it clear. It was the first indication I ever had that there *were* leagues."

"I thought Vicki Brickner was your first love," Hannah said.

Gad laughed—it always delighted him to hear her mention by name, as casually as if she knew them, people from his past—and said, "Vicki was my first girlfriend. Another matter altogether."

Hannah imitated him: "'Brilliant, gorgeous, sexy, impulsive Vicki Brickner—much too good for me. And she was even musical!' So what ever happened to *her*, anyway?"

"She finally figured that out," he said. "She found someone who *was* good enough for her, first year away at college, and later they got married. Last I heard they were still deliriously happy together—the husband's some kind of local left-wing politician, very glamorous himself, and she gave up a great job to stay home with their kid"—he'd heard this from Antar, who by chance lived two blocks from Vicki and her family in Chelsea and ran into her from time to time buying groceries in D'Agostino—"and supposedly the kid's even better looking and smarter than Vicki was when we knew her."

"Bad luck," Hannah said. "If she'd married you—"

"She would've left me by now," Gad finished for her, and although he had meant this to be a joke, he was assaulted suddenly by a vision—it ran through his mind like a snippet of film in fast-motion—of an alternate universe in which he and Vicki *had* married and lived happily together. The handsome and intelligent child was their son. They lived in New York, of course—in his vision the three of them were emerging from a building, holding hands. Vicki looked exactly as she'd looked when he'd last seen her: tough, beautiful, in wire-rimmed sunglasses and a denim jacket and square-toed Frye boots. He looked serene, more handsome than usual. He was a wildly successful composer.

"Why would anyone leave you?" The seriousness with which Hannah asked this question shut off his vision so abruptly he saw the screen go white, flecked with odd-shaped, flickering bits of black, and heard the *flap flap* as the film slipped off the spool.

"Why would anyone leave me?" he repeated. "Hannah, you're ...." He shook his head, laughing helplessly. What had he done, he asked himself, to cause her to see him this way? Fleetingly, an urge came over him to tell her the one secret he had kept from her. He had never consciously decided not to tell her anything about his infidelities; he had merely skipped them, he thought, as he told her, bit by bit, the "story of his life" that she demanded. But now that it had come into his mind that he might—that he should—confess, he hesitated. *Was* there good cause—any cause—to make this confession, when he knew that it would disappoint her? (For he had no doubt it would—and he had no doubt such disappointment in him would change things between them. Ruin things? Perhaps. Perhaps.)

He said, fecklessly—and so quietly that it was possible she couldn't hear him—"People leave each other all the time, for all sorts of reasons," and then (pure luck!), seeing that they were approaching one of the paths' few crossroads, set a firm hand on her elbow and said, "Let's go this way, shall we?"

And as soon as they had made their turn, he changed the subject. "So," he said, "did you notice the latest addition at dinner tonight? The blond in pink and pearls?"

"The novelist," Hannah said.

"A novelist?" Gad said. "Really? All that makeup! Hot pink lipstick, stuff around the eyes. And that Southern drawl!—I could swear she was putting it on. I've never heard anything like it. And did you happen to notice that our other Southerner, that old dame—I know, she's a poet, right, and sort of famous?"—Hannah nodded vigorously—"ignored her totally? So what do you think: is she for real, or what?"

"The novelist?" Hannah laughed. Then she astonished him by assuring him, in rapid succession, that the Southern drawl, extravagant as it was, was perfectly authentic, that it had its origins in a small town outside Montgomery, Alabama, that the writer's name was Daisy Appleby, and that her first novel, though it "wasn't very good" (it was not only a "mishmash of up-to-the-minute troubles: wife abuse, date rape, and recovered memories of incest," it was also "the most superficial example of Southern Gothic" she'd ever read), "did have something going for it. You can tell that even though she's shallow and misguided and sort of crass, she's serious about writing and even talented. She hasn't much to say, but she's very interested in saying it and sometimes she says it in fairly interesting ways. So, to answer—"

"You didn't even talk to her," Gad interrupted. "When did you find out all this?"

"I've read her book."

"But you didn't even—"

"And the flap copy. That's how I know where she's from. She doesn't live there anymore; she's one of those itinerant creative writing teachers—a year here, a year there. Either she can't keep a job or she likes the variety." Gad blinked at her. "Anyhow, to answer your question: yes, I'd say she's the real thing, in her way."

"Sometimes you astound me, Hannah."

Hannah bowed her head. "As you do me."

In the morning, Gad reconsidered Daisy Appleby. Even from across the room, he could see that she'd put on a fresh coat of pink lipstick. None of the women here wore lipstick—not *while* they were here, anyway, Gad allowed. Certainly none of them showed up in the dining room in cashmere cardigans and pearls or dresses. This morning Daisy Appleby was in a dress—black-and-white polka dots—and though Gad could not be sure, he was betting that when she stood up it would reveal itself to be a minidress. Probably skin-tight, too.

She was causing a commotion among the men, he could see that. She was the lone woman at her table and the men encircling her seemed to be striving mightily to outdo one another to amuse her. Their voices were very loud; every gesture seemed exaggerated. And Daisy *was* amused, or putting on a good performance of it. She kept throwing her head back, laughing and lifting her hands as if to beg them to show her some mercy. Cascades of dramatically blond hair, in long S-shaped curls, fell over the back of her chair. It occurred to him that her hair was so elaborately arranged around her face and shoulders she must have had to do something to it before appearing in public. How early would she have had to wake up to manage that before their early breakfast? He almost asked Hannah, but decided that she would be no more likely to know than he would. Besides, he had a strong feeling that she wouldn't like the question. There were certain things it was all right to speculate about: "matters of public record" was how

Gad put it, teasing her (this category, she had told him, so sol-
emnly he'd felt he had no choice *but* to tease her, included where
people were from, what their work was like, aspects of their
personalities as implied/suggested by their artists' statements
and other published autobiographical musings, and whether
they were "serious" or not). There was a much broader category of things about which she said that it was "unbecom-
ing" to make guesses. Anything even remotely "personal," he
knew, fell into this latter class. What Daisy Appleby did or
didn't do to her hair, how it was done, or how long it took to
do it (ditto her outlined, shadowed eyes and long pink claws)
was, he was pretty sure, off-limits. He was *absolutely* sure that
if Hannah divined that right now he was trying to make up
his mind which of the men gathered around Daisy Appleby
was likely to succeed with her first, she would disapprove severely. Thus he nodded now as Hannah talked about a new
book she'd begun to read last night in bed—stories she admired, with certain reservations—and, between bites of
oatmeal, sneaking glances back at Daisy's table, he ranked the
men silently. He gave first place to the soulful-looking ab-
stract painter who'd arrived a week or so ago. The second
spot he bestowed upon the young sculptor whose mother was
always calling from Omaha during dinner (it had become
quite a joke among the others), as he was very handsome and
earnest, and Gad suspected that when she tired of the
painter—whom she appeared just now to be favoring—she
would seek an antidote to his morose, if sexually charged,
world-weary style. Gad was weighing another sculptor—
less spirited, not nearly so handsome and much older than
the boy whose mother called so often, but more forceful and
entertaining—against a short story writer Hannah had said
was "nearly a genius," whose social awkwardness made Gad
almost like him from afar (the artfully shaggy hair and beard
and the sad, wistful eyes and smile would be in his favor, too,
Gad thought, with women) for third place—reflecting that the

sculptor Keech would have easily nabbed this spot if he were still here; thank God he wasn't—when Hannah caught him. She rapped his knuckles with the back of her teaspoon. "I'm disappointed in you," she said. "They're probably all married, you know. Except maybe the one who gets those phone calls. And *she* definitely is. To her second husband, I believe. A very good writer, older, with a hugely inflated ego. Or so his interviews would suggest."

Gad didn't even pause to wonder how she'd learned to read his mind. "How come it's all right to hazard guesses about who's married and who's not? That's pretty personal."

"I don't agree," said Hannah. "It's a matter—"

"Ah, right. Of public record. Of course. A legal, contractual—"

"They should all be ashamed of themselves," Hannah said, so sternly he was abashed. Had it had never crossed her mind, he asked himself, that people assumed *they* were having an affair? He had no doubt that this was what was generally thought (for what else would they think? What did these people know about real feeling, real human connections?), but while he was amused when he caught people smiling knowingly as they watched him and Hannah talking, or when whispered conversation ceased as soon as their presence was noted—Hannah, it occurred to him for the first time, would be outraged. He had had the idea that they never spoke of this because between them there was a silent agreement that even to mention it would be beneath them. But as he studied Hannah now, as she watched the painter Gad was betting on to come in first, who was telling what must be a joke (which apparently required the inscription, with an outstretched index finger, of a series of straight lines and circles and other, more abstruse delineations in the air), he understood that he'd been wrong: that Hannah was so far superior to all of them— to him as well—that it would simply not have entered into her thoughts that such gossip, base as it was, existed.

She turned to him, inclining her head toward the tableful of supplicants. "Imbeciles," she said.

Gad snickered uneasily. "Didn't you once tell me that the bashful, shaggy-looking one was brilliant?"

"At writing," Hannah said. "One thing has nothing to do with the other. And they may even be mutually exclusive. This place makes you wonder, doesn't it?"

"It does, yes."

"And *you*," Hannah said. She pointed a finger, encircled by the ring that matched her eyes, and wagged it at him. "You shouldn't waste your time contemplating such idiocy."

"Well. . .no. I shouldn't." He laughed, this time unequivocally. "Still. . .it's only human."

"Sure it is," she said. Sharply. "So is chewing with your mouth open. But that doesn't mean it's attractive." She scraped back her chair and began to gather up her breakfast dishes.

"Time to go to work?"

"Unless you want to sit around watching the reprobates all day."

He didn't; to work they went.

Considering the inauspicious start (indeed, there was a corner of his mind in which he kept on fretting over Hannah's scolding for most of the morning, even as he worked in what he imagined were the three remaining clean, uncluttered corners), and therefore his low expectations of this day—his thirty-fifth, he noted, at the Colony (and thus Hannah's twenty-first)—he was thoroughly amazed to discover that by midafternoon he'd finished the third movement and thus the whole concerto.

He hadn't known he was so close. In fact he suspected that he hadn't been, but that an unforeseen and inexplicable burst of "creative energy" or inspiration, notions he'd been known to ridicule ("Euphemisms," he would say, "for the combination of plain, rigorous hard work, proper concentration, and the straightforward application of one's talents and intelligence required for the making of a work of art"), had come to him (in spite, he wondered, or somehow because of Hannah's lecture?) on this day and carried him along, pushing him well past what he believed he could accomplish in a single day even in "Artland"—Hannah's name, of late, not for the Colony at large but for the place they had made for themselves in it.

He nearly fled his studio and raced to hers to tell her. But he checked himself, for one of the Colony's few rules forbade unbidden visits during working hours—and this, he'd felt from the start, was a just rule: it was one he shouldn't break. So instead he paced and muttered, tensely humming bits of the concerto, staying in the studio as long as he could bear it, then returning to his bedroom, where he paced the five feet between the bed and the door, still humming and muttering, for another half hour and then fussed in the communal bathroom for much longer than necessary, changed his clothes (traded one pair of faded jeans, one white tee shirt, and one denim shirt for another, for no reason except to pass the time) and crossed, fifty minutes early, to the Colony's main building, to sit on the edge of an armchair in the commons room and flip through a series of literary magazines, his eyes on the door. Each time it opened he stood, then sat, when someone came in who was not Hannah.

By the time she came, just before the dinner bell rang, he was too annoyed—irrationally, he knew—to tell her straight out. When she asked, cheerfully, how his day had gone—obviously, hers had gone well too—he shrugged. "Very well, thanks," he said curtly. "Yours?" She was too happy to notice and she launched into a gleeful account of a new cycle of poems that had "seemed to come out of nowhere." She'd had such a good day she'd had trouble stopping—she'd even considered working right through dinner. "But I knew that I'd miss you. I decided that it wasn't worth it—the poems will still be there in the morning."

He couldn't stand it; he broke down—telling himself he was an idiot even to think of it as "breaking down"—and gave her his news. She clapped and jumped up and down like a child not even old enough to be in school who'd just been told she would be taken on an outing. She hugged him, smacked his arm, then grabbed hold of the arm that she had slapped and made him promise that immediately after dinner he would take her to his studio and play it for her.

This he did. He was very nervous, sitting at the piano; even after he began to play he felt his anxiety running through him forcefully, a current. He tried not to look at Hannah, who for her part could not seem to be still. It was strange to be at the piano with someone fluttering about it, touching things—strange to have someone with him in the studio at all. And was she even listening?

Apparently. When he was through, in the silence that seemed so abrupt and so profound he felt as if a switch had been thrown, a silence that felt like the absence of not only sound but also light (and air, his own breath—everything), she came to the piano bench and sat down beside him. "It's beautiful," she said. She touched his right hand, which like his left was still curled in the air above the keys. "It's just beautiful."

Hannah lifted her hand and withdrew it. He let his fall to his lap. "Do you really think so?" Hannah nodded. "It's terrifying," he said.

She didn't say *What is?* "I know," she said.

But he wasn't sure what he had meant. He closed his eyes but he could not recapture that instant before she'd joined him—that sliver of blackness, of nothingness, between the lifting of his fingers from the piano and the touch of Hannah's hand on his. When he opened his eyes, she was watching him so steadily and with such tenderness he drew her toward him without thinking. His arms enfolded her in a way that seemed both complicated and familiar, as if she were a package with a complex shape he knew by heart.

Wrapped in his arms, Hannah seemed to shift and sigh, then settle there. He felt her heart beating against his chest, her hair like feathers everywhere it touched his skin—his cheek, his neck, his hands. They were both very still; it took him a moment before he realized that he was holding his breath. Then he felt Hannah's arms slip underneath his, lift and come around his shoulders weightlessly, and he exhaled. They kissed.

The slide from the piano bench onto the rug below, the slow rolling progress over the small field the faded many-colored oval made between the bench's legs—square-ended, pegged (briefly Gad faced one of them up close, his forehead pressed to its pockmarked veneer)—and the sharp metal multi-jointed legs that led up to the cot against the wall, the climb upwards and the spilling over onto the thin quilt that covered the thin mattress and one flat exhausted pillow—all of this, for Gad, was accompanied by a disjunct, contrapuntal tumbling-out of memory: of faces, mouths, closed eyes, and hair that wasn't Hannah's as he slid his fingers through it. Closing his own eyes, he even thought (delirious!) he heard someone come in, whisper, "Don't!" But Hannah's skin, Hannah herself, as clothes were tugged and twisted, shed—as he felt against him Hannah's shoulders, bare arms, breasts, hips, belly, thighs, the bottoms of her cool bare feet—seemed to him something he could slip inside, and once there, nothing, nobody could follow him. Thus—*there*, thought Gad; perhaps he even said it—was the monitory specter banished. *There*. As was the olio of not-Hannahs. *There*, thought Gad. *There*.

When they separated, by the inch or two the cot allowed, Gad sought the words to summon up the wonderment he felt, the sense of revelation and yet confirmation mixed together, as if one did not, should not contradict the other, and he raised himself up on one elbow—he was about to comment first (jokingly, gently) on their silence: had they ever spent so much time in each other's company without a single word passing between them?—but he saw then how strange Hannah looked, how pale. He reached out for her with his free hand—touched her chin with two fingers—but before he could ask her what was wrong, she burst into tears.

He was astonished. He tried to pull her toward him but she shook off his hand as soon as it touched her arm. His astonishment gave way to alarm, and then—when she continued to weep—to bewilderment. She gave no sign that she might stop crying anytime soon. Cautiously he reached out again, and since she did not swipe his hand away he stroked her hair and said—what was he to say?—"There, there."

She kept on weeping. Bafflement now made way for simple dismay and finally for irritation. "Hannah," he began, "why don't—" But she reached up and put her hand over his mouth. A theatrical gesture. If her sobbing had been less heartfelt and pathetic he might have thought she was playing a part. He had to make an effort to control his annoyance as he peeled her hand from his mouth.

The weeping continued. It had begun to transform her. Her face was swollen and looked raw, the skin streaked viciously with red. For twenty minutes or so this kept on, and with nothing to do but wait for her to finish, when she'd stopped at last he realized that even his impatience had fled and he was only bored. She sat up, pulled her knees to her chest, and began to talk. At first she spoke in fragments, still gasping and sniffling, and he couldn't make out any of it. But then he understood that she was talking about Saint John, about how guilty she felt. "Guilty," she said, "and *wrong.*"

"Not about *this*—don't misunderstand"—she fished out her flannel shirt from underneath her and pressed one of its sleeves to her nose—"well, no, that isn't right. About this too. Of course about this—about you." She looked at him miserably. Her nose was still running and the puffed-up pockets below her eyes looked boiled. His inability to pity her, when she was so pitiable, made him so uncomfortable he turned away. "All these years I've kept imagining that I'd grow out of it, that it was a limitation in me. But it only gets worse."

"What does?" he asked, as gently as he could.

But instead of answering, she began to ramble, talking about Saint John. How *good* he was. How deserving. How she wasn't worthy of him—"and not because of *this*," she said, "although this only proves it."

"Proves what, exactly?"

She wasn't listening to him. Clutching her checked shirt to her chest, she was going on and on about how kind, how reliable, how high-minded her fiancé was. And—her voice dropped to a whisper—how bored she was by him. By everything about him. *Especially* his goodness.

Gad knew he mustn't laugh or make a joke about this. But what *should* he say? This was hardly the moment to propose that she reconsider her plans to marry the guy. Perhaps if they got dressed. He tried to think of a polite way to suggest this, as Hannah kept on about Saint John's probity, his "obvious" superiority to all other mortals, and her shameful, dreadful—"sinful," she actually said once—lack of proper feeling for him. As if it were a sin to be bored.

"And now *this*," she said.

"This meaning me." He felt vaguely, delicately offended, though he wasn't sure if this was because he'd been reduced to a finishing touch or because somewhere in all of this was an implication that he wasn't boring—therefore wasn't "good." He murmured, "I do the best I can."

Hannah, however, was still lost in her own circular thoughts: nothing he had to say was of interest right now. Round and round she went—rectitude, boredom, and guilt—and round again. Her moral failings, her fiancé's perfection, his tiresomeness, her guilt again. Et cetera.

His own boredom, as he listened, seemed to him something he could have offered up to her only a short time ago as a choice bit of irony over which they would have laughed together. Instead—such was the power of circumstances—it was something (the first thing!) he would have to keep from her, the first thought or feeling he had ever had regarding her that would have to be kept a secret.

And the thought that followed this one, creeping in on tiptoes, was the second: how grateful he was that he had just one week of his residency left.

Hannah had lapsed into silence. She held her balled-up shirt against her chest with both hands, her chin resting on it. He thought it might be all right for him to sit up now, and perhaps if he began to dress, she would too. He raised himself cautiously, reaching down with one hand for his socks, his eyes on Hannah. She didn't move or make a sound and he took this as permission.

As he put on his clothes, he kept an eye on her, covertly. He wasn't sure what he expected, or feared, that she would do next, but there was no sense taking any chances. For an instant, thinking this way, he felt like a tough guy—*Don't let the dame out of your sight. Who knows what she'll pull?*—but immediately after this he felt foolish, embarrassed; he had to look away from her puffy eyes and jaw (it looked almost as if someone had slugged her), her hair in mournful strings that drooped over her naked shoulders. He was reminded all at once of something Janet had said to him long ago, when he was in the midst of one of his outbursts of contrition: that she'd begun to find what she had once considered his "adorable remorse" so unattractive she could not recall what his appeal to her had ever been.

He forced himself to speak, to break the spell, for how long could they remain here, neither of them speaking, in his studio (*his* for another week, then someone else's—this, he foresaw suddenly, would not be so easy for him to accede to), a little cabin hidden from the thirty or so others by the hundred-foot-tall paper birches, maples, balsam firs and hemlocks that surrounded it; how long could he stand here fully clothed beside the piano contemplating Hannah sitting naked on the cot, the red-and-black crushed checkerboard of flannel shirt (damp now, no doubt, and smeared with mucus) held tightly over her small breasts? He cleared his throat. He said, first, with the constrained cheer of a kindergarten teacher, or a nurse, "*Here* you are!" as he handed her her underpants and jeans. It was only now that he saw that the underpants were silky, pond green, bordered with a band of lace, and that the jeans were patched on both knees with what must have been upholstery fabric, gold and white brocade, and neatly sewn on with gold thread—details that inexplicably filled *him* with grief. As Hannah took the things he offered, he said (somewhat desperately, he thought, but it was what had come into his mind and now he found that he could think of nothing else), "Tell me about the new poems."

She seemed taken aback. She stared at him as if she couldn't remember what poems he meant. Perhaps for the moment she really had forgotten. But then a tiny, pale, shy-looking smile—an escapee from her sadness, against orders, Gad thought—broke out, and, with frequent pauses and at first with sentences that trailed off after a few words or shifted midway and turned into other sentences, she began to tell him about the poems she had begun that day, the ones she'd mentioned before dinner, "before"—the shy smile again, unseen until tonight—"you told me about finishing the concerto."

She'd worked feverishly all day—"and I mean that literally," she said. "It was just as if I had a fever." She'd felt hot and dizzy. "I was in a *state.*" And she'd had to hurry, writing, because for the first time in her life, she told him, half a dozen different poems "were coming" at the same time. Stranger still, they were unlike any poems she'd ever written before.

"Unlike them how?" he asked. By now she was standing up too, putting on her clothes, and as she dressed and talked about her work, she was coming slowly back to herself. It seemed all right to ask a question.

"I don't know exactly how to describe it. For one
thing, they were coming in all these different voices. So that
even though I was getting lines for six different poems at once,
I could tell without even having to think about it which ones
belonged where, because the voices—oh." She interrupted
herself, pausing in the buttoning of her wrinkled, snotty shirt.
"I forgot. You hate it when I talk about poems 'coming' to
me." She struck a pose, imitating him— right hand on chin,
left index finger in the air—and said, in a deep, put-on voice
that was nothing like his: "'Rigor, concentration, talent. Nothing just *comes*, Hannah. There's no mystery about it."

"That's awful," he said.

"That's what I keep telling you."

"I mean the impersonation."

She didn't laugh at this, but she smiled, which was
good enough for now.

"Actually," he said, "today, I must admit, I had to
wonder." She cocked her head expectantly. "You know," he
said. "About the whole enterprise. It all seemed more myste-
rious than usual."

"Is that so?" She was grinning at him now. "That's good."

"Yes. Probably it is." He grinned back at her. She'd
finished buttoning her shirt. All covered up, she looked almost exactly like herself again. "You still haven't told me what
the poems are like," he said.

"I don't think can," she said. "I'll just have to read
them to you when they're done."

"I hope you will," he said.

"Of course I will." The smile he knew. Hannah. Re-
lief flooded him as if it had been injected into a vein. "I'll tell
you one thing," she said. "There are all these voices in all these
different but obviously related poems, and every single damn
one of them is talking about. . .oh, about making good, or re-
forming, or overcoming something. It's all extrication and lib-
eration, you know? So all day I'm sitting there thinking of this

group of poems as the 'redemption cycle.'" One eyebrow lifted—a gesture he knew well. "So do you think that's sufficiently pretentious, or what?"

"Not at all," Gad said. "Personally, I'm a big fan of redemption."

Hannah laughed—a full-throated, merry, wonderful laugh, as unexpected, as metamorphic as the outburst of tears had been.

"You know," she said seriously, after a moment, "you ought to try letting your work go off in some new direction. While you still have some time. You've finished everything you'd hoped to do here. You could use the time you have left to experiment, to try something altogether different—out of character. Something you'd never do otherwise."

"I might," he said. And it was an appealing idea, although he wasn't sure just what it would entail. "Actually, I might. Why not?"

"Why not is right. What do you have to lose?"

They considered each other. They were standing no more than a yard apart on the rug that lay between the piano and the cot. He glanced down at their feet, in socks, on the rug—his dark blue, hers polka dotted, pink on black—and her eyes followed. She laughed. Then he did.

Afterwards he could not have said who had reached for whom, or even how (had one pulled the other toward him or herself? Had one of them fallen into the other's arms?), but their kiss, which followed naturally, lasted a long time, and when it was over both of them were smiling. Gad felt relieved and elated at the same time—a mix that left him light-headed. Hannah's smile was serene but otherwise unreadable. Her eyes were dry.

"You know what we ought to do?" Gad said. "We ought to take a break tomorrow afternoon and go into town and buy a bottle of champagne. We should have a celebration."

"Should we?" She was still smiling at him.

"Absolutely. We should." He was nodding, he realized, as vigorously as the thrift-shop doll, a little Dutch boy with a bunch of tulips in his left hand, that Janet kept on their car's dashboard ("so that there'll always be somebody here who agrees with me"). He made himself stop. He hated that doll's head-bobbing. "We have to celebrate my finishing the concerto, don't we? And we should celebrate these new poems of yours."

"But they're not done. I've just gotten started on them."

"Still. We should celebrate *that*—your having begun something so new to you. We should be celebrating your adventuresomeness."

"My adventuresomeness," Hannah repeated. Then she nodded; then—surprising him—she laughed. "All right, but only if we reserve a toast for your intention to start something new too, something so different from what you've ever tried to do before that you won't know what *you're* doing either."

"Did I say I'd do that?"

"Sure you did."

"Oh, did I, really?" Gad began to laugh. "Well, why not? Why the hell not?" Laughing, he took her two hands in his. They felt cool and extraordinarily small. And he felt expansive—he *felt* as if he could start something new and daring, something altogether different from anything he'd ever even thought of doing; he felt he could do it right now.

"Tomorrow then," said Hannah.

"Tomorrow."

And when tomorrow came, she reminded him at breakfast—she looked gay and mischievous—that he "mustn't have the faintest idea" what he was doing. "That's the central thing," she said. "If you find yourself wandering into familiar territory, start over. Start fresh."

He still wasn't entirely sure what this meant, but in

his studio he took her dictum as seriously as he could. He sat at the piano and experimented—"fooled around," as he told Hannah when they met as planned, right after lunch, for their excursion into town. The odd thing, he reported, was that even though nothing had come of it ("Not *yet*," Hannah interjected), he'd enjoyed himself as he had not in years. Hannah nodded sagely. "And you?" he asked. "How are the redeemers?"

"Coming along," she said. "Chattering and interrupting one another. You know those stories where there are a bunch of men sitting around in an inn, telling their troubles as the samovar merrily boils away? This morning that's what they reminded me of. Every one of them thinks his or her confession is the most interesting."

"And you're the boiling kettle?" Gad said.

Hannah laughed. "I guess."

They bought their bottle of champagne and then wandered through the little town from store to store, buying fruit and chocolate and expensive crackers—treats, they decided, that they'd keep in Gad's studio. A plan was forming; they talked it over as they stood before a bin of yellow apples, choosing. They would take a break from now on every day. Together, sometime after lunch—at Gad's, because Hannah liked it there, she said: she liked the look of all those yellow cards spread out as if a hand of poker had just come to a showdown. Her studio, she told him—she held an apple in each hand, weighing one against the other—was so tidy it looked as if nobody worked there. "I'm so bad that when I type up a new draft of a poem, I immediately put it in a desk drawer." If there was clutter anywhere around her—if there was even one thing out of place—she was unable to work. She was addicted to bare surfaces, she said. And yet the signs of his work, in his studio, were pleasing to her. They delighted her. And why was that? he asked. They had paid for their apples, oranges, and pears and moved across the street, to the town's one small hardware store. They were walking down the housewares aisle, looking for glasses they might use for their champagne. She liked the contrast, Hannah said—it made her feel hopeful. He considered saying, "Full of hope about what?" but decided not to say anything. He had the feeling that Hannah's preference for his studio was less lofty than she made it sound, that what was really on her mind was that his presence in hers, even for an hour or two each day, would spoil things for her there. But even if this were true, he realized that he didn't mind; he liked the idea of her coming to see him, of keeping treats there for her visits.

They went back to the Colony, to his studio. It was late by then—too late, they agreed, to get any work done before dinner. Gad sat on the piano bench, Hannah on the wooden swivel chair he never used. They opened the champagne and drank it out of the triangular-topped cocktail glasses that had been the only stemware they could find, and when they made love this time Gad was conscious of how lovely she was and how fragile. They both slept then for a little while, facing each other on the narrow cot, their legs entangled and their foreheads touching. He woke up first and stroked her hair to wake her; she smiled even before she opened her eyes.

They were both slightly drunk, and when they stood up to get dressed, they stumbled and had to hold onto each other. Hannah was unusually quiet as they dressed, but her eyes were dry—Gad kept a close watch on her—and she wasn't sad, he thought. Walking back through the woods together, they held hands tightly, like children in a fairy tale.

Thereafter they met every day at two. They would sit on the floor and drink tea and take tiny bites of chocolate, peel an orange and pass it back and forth between them, each pulling off a section, and talk about how their mornings had gone. They would share an apple or a pear. Then he might play for her a fragment—it was all fragments—of what he was "working on." He thought of it that way, in quotes. Was he working, really? He spent his mornings fooling around at the piano in a way he hadn't since he was eleven or twelve years old. Hannah approved. She egged him on. She applauded every disconnected, nonsensical fragment he offered up to her. Somehow this made him laugh. It seemed to him that his hours at the piano were filled now with a sort of abandon and joy that must have marked his earliest experiences with it—that this was what had turned him into who and what he was.

Hannah reported daily on the progress of the new poems. She read them to him as they were completed, one at a time. She was working on them singly now that she'd "collected all the lines" for all of them. She would polish each one fiercely—even Gad, who knew nothing much about poetry, could tell that these poems had been barrel-tumbled, cut and shined until they gleamed: they dazzled him. After she had read the newest poem aloud, she'd read them all, once more, in the order that she'd settled on that day. Every day she rearranged them. Even Gad could tell that the order made a difference, and that every poem she added to the mix changed the entire cycle.

He loved listening to her read. She assumed a different voice when she spoke each poem; she referred to the "speakers" in each one the way he had on the day they'd gone to town—her redeemers, she called them, although she wondered aloud if the word was exactly right when they weren't saving anybody but themselves. "Expiators would be more precise. But the sound of it's so ugly."

She was searching for a title for the whole of the cycle. She'd rejected "Redemption" and although she flirted with "Redeemers" for a day, she concluded that it was too imprecise. "Confessions?" she asked Gad, and answered before he could: "No. Too simple-minded."

Even if he only listened, marveling, as Hannah freeassociated, listing and rejecting possibilities, it pleased him to be part of this. He'd never given any thought to titles himself;

he'd only once gone beyond a number and key signature, and then reluctantly, at the insistence of the chamber group for which he'd written the piece (which he named, sarcastically, "The Prachtvoll Galantuomo Sonata," and was amazed when no objections to this mishmash of the languages he'd studied at Wesleyan, and remembered only spottily, were raised). But now he was thinking seriously about titling both the concerto (in G minor, for piano and orchestra) and the sinfonietta (in D major), for it was very pleasant to sit in his studio with Hannah, sipping tea and taking thoughtful bites of cracker as they talked about the "mood" or "spirit," the nature and the meaning of what he had written. He began his own lists of possibilities, with Hannah's help.

They embraced only after everything else: after conversation, tea and chocolate, fruit and crackers, the exchange of work and the discussion of it, their list-making and so on. Then he would put a tape on—something he had chosen especially for her: Liszt's "Transcendental Études," a recording of seventeenth century hymns, Beethoven's works for piano, violin, and cello—and they would move to the small cot together. Afterwards they would lie quietly for a while before they both returned to work for an hour or two before dinner.

One afternoon, as a lark, after they dressed, they sat down at the piano and wrote a canon together. In half an hour they had it. Since it was meant to be sung as a round for three voices, they couldn't sing it properly, but they sang the twelve measures through together as a straightforward song, sitting side by side on the piano bench. "It's wonderful," said Hannah, and Gad laughed because she sounded so bewildered. "It is," he agreed. It was—it was a very pretty song and they had hammered it out somehow in no time.

They made clean copies of it on two of his yellow cards: he wrote out the music, she added the lyrics, and across the top of each card Gad wrote "Little Canon, a tre," and Hannah reprinted, just below that, the first lyric line—"Spring comes at last in these woods."

As the week wore on, Hannah finished what she was now tentatively calling "Amends" and had begun to split her days between new work, for which she reserved the morning, and finishing the poems she'd started earlier in her stay—she'd paused to count them and was shocked to find that she had amassed complete unpolished drafts of more than twenty poems—in the hours both after lunch, before their daily break together, and afterwards.

For his part, Gad decided that what he was working on these days was a symphonic ode, or something along those lines. The music itself was rather baroque, he realized with some amusement (so that was what came of letting himself go!) and it was still in bits and pieces that so far seemed much more conflicted than unified, but he was beginning, he thought, to see the shadow of a pattern emerging among them—indeed, he told Hannah, a pattern that looked something like an argument. He told her he would dedicate it to her if he ever finished it, and Hannah said, "An argument? You're going to dedicate an argument to me?" and then she laughed, so that he knew she was joking. He didn't say what he felt—that she had inspired him. There was a line, he thought, that ought not to be crossed between them. He thought of all the times he'd said "I love you" to the women with whom he had found himself entangled and how hard it was to take it back—how often and how hopelessly someone had said, "But you *said* . . . ." and how he'd had no recourse but to say, "I meant it when I said it, but now . . ." (shrugging, wondering if he *had* meant it and why he could not remember having felt it). But he was ashamed of himself, for this wasn't fair to Hannah, who asked nothing of him, who had never once so much as implied that she expected them to keep in touch once he had left the Colony. They would resume their lives and they would recall each other fondly. He could not imagine anything ugly passing between them.

He said, in atonement for his thoughts, "I would never have begun this—whatever it turns out to be—without you. You know that." And he was both gratified and unsettled that she looked so pleased.

And then—quite abruptly, it seemed—it *was* time for him to leave. Hannah stood outside the phone booth as he made arrangements for a taxi to pick him up in the morning and take him to the airport. He tried to haggle over the price— it was a long, expensive trip—while Hannah made faces at him from the other side of the glass. They were both acting as if nothing unusual were happening. All through dinner they had talked and joked and pointedly ignored the others as they always did. He thought once, for the first time, of what meals would be like for her for the next two weeks, when he was gone, but quickly he shut down this line of thinking. She would manage, he told himself firmly. *She* wasn't worried, after all, was she? She'd given him no indication that she was. She was friendly, she was charming—more than charming, delightful. She was clever and funny. If she chose to, she'd make friends.

He surveyed the commons room as they walked through it now. The others were milling about, waiting for the evening's presentation to begin. Daisy Appleby was going to read from her new novel—*A Very Pretty Girl*, it was called, according to the flyer Gad had found in his mailbox this morning. It had made him laugh. You had to hand it to her: she was self-satisfied as hell. Audacious. Examining the flyer, he'd felt mildly curious, for he'd watched her and her admirers on and off at meals (he believed that his ranking had been close to perfect, for although he seemed to have been wrong about the ingenuous young sculptor—he was too sanguine to have been through what appeared to be a mill—all the others had that hangdog look that suggested they'd been used up and discarded. Indeed, she'd made it through the whole list with astonishing speed) and he couldn't help wondering if any of her escapades here were making their way into what he assumed would be overstated, dressed-up autobiography. But Hannah hadn't even mentioned it, and when Daisy reappeared now in the commons room—she'd left in a hurry before dinner was quite over—having changed her clothes, wearing something that looked like a cat suit made of stretchy white lace, skin tight and covering her from her neck down to her ankles, white lace gloves and white high heels, Gad realized that most of his curiosity was already satisfied.

He glanced around once more as he held the door open for Hannah. They were going to his studio; she'd offered to help him pack up. Was there anyone among those gathered here who would not be pleased to count her among their acquaintances? he demanded of himself. But the tremor that passed through him then suggested that this was another route down which he'd do better not to go. It wasn't any of his business, anyway, he reminded himself. She had two weeks in which to do as she wished. *He* was going home.

He didn't talk to her as they walked to the studio, and after a few minutes she gave up trying to engage him in a conversation. By the time they got there, he was gloomier than he had any right to be. Hannah raised an eyebrow when he started tossing things in boxes without saying anything, but she joined in, and they worked in silence until the boxes that he'd unpacked in this room six weeks ago were full again.

Hannah sat down on the cot and patted the space beside her. Gad sat down, feeling foolish. He was not exactly sad, he told himself, so much as uneasy. Hannah took his hand and he was afraid she was about to make a speech; to keep her from doing so, he made himself speak first, saying whatever came into his head—one thing after another, too quickly, talking about nothing (when would the staff come in to clean the studio? would the weather be all right for flying in the morning? could they manage these three boxes in the dark tonight, or should they come back early in the morning for them?)—and not waiting for her to respond to any of his questions.

One part of his mind, despite his chattering, kept worrying. But he couldn't even pinpoint what the trouble was, precisely: his disquiet and his apprehensiveness—his dread—were that diffuse. He could not even recall the last time he had written to or heard from Janet, and the city where they lived, which by default he was obliged to call "home" though he'd never thought of it that way, and to which he would return tomorrow (and from which he might escape again *when?* Never, he thought. Never in a million years would Janet stand for this again, not when he hadn't been able to bring himself to call her *once* since he'd been here), he could not think of a single reason to rejoice in landing in ten hours from now. And his dread of that moment, his "homecoming"—and of all the moments afterwards!—was mixed up, he knew, with his uneasiness about his leaving here, and leaving Hannah—leaving Hannah here without him. His mind ran in circles: leaving and returning, in dismay about them both.

He sat looking around him, dazed—silent now, at last. Hannah was silent too, and he was grateful to her for that. He noticed that on the small desk by the window there were two apples and an orange. He should send Hannah "home" with them, he thought; he was loathe to leave them for his replacement (his replacement! His eyes filmed over unexpectedly at this thought, at the very idea of someone else laying claim to his cabin, which felt more like home to him than the house he had been living in for the last decade). "Take what's left of—" he began, when Hannah at the same time said, as brightly as if she intended it to be a joke, "We should never have met."

He turned to her. He couldn't read her face—*was* she joking? Was he supposed to say, "Of course we should have"? Or was he *meant* to take this as a joke, and to respond in kind? (Which would be how, exactly? "Ah, but alas we did, my dear"—facetious melodrama?) Or did she just want him to say, "You're right"? He had years—decades—of experience responding the wrong way to Janet, who almost always seemed to have in mind what his response to her should be (he'd answer her and she'd groan, "Can't you just say . . ." and fill in what she had expected—*needed*, she said—from him). It seemed urgently important to him now to figure out precisely what Hannah required of him. But the harder he thought about it—and as the silence following what she had said stretched out between them—the more lost he felt. He bowed his head.

"You don't have to say anything," said Hannah, just as if she'd heard what he was thinking. "It's hard to know what to say, isn't it?" He looked up at her and the gratitude and wonder that rushed through him threatened to resolve itself in tears. But she wasn't crying, and although she sounded sad there wasn't anything about her voice or manner or expression that suggested that she would cry, and he was damned if he would be the one to weep while she looked on or patted him and said, "There, there." He shrugged, and Hannah suddenly withdrew her hand from his and brought both of her hands to his face, pulled it close to hers, and said, this time without a trace of *allégresse*, "You understand, don't you, that we're parting forever?"

This time he did not even think of answering: he understood it wasn't necessary. Instead, after a moment during which she held his face in her hands and looked at him steadily and sadly, and throughout which he held his breath (the memory of that first night, when she'd sobbed and he had felt so distant from her, waiting coldly for her to "pull herself together," still a disturbance to him—although whether his dread was on behalf of her or of himself was not at all clear to him), he closed what little space there was between them and kissed her. When he drew back, just far enough so that he could see what the effect of this had been, she looked so sorrowful he couldn't think of what to do except kiss her again.

In the morning, after they had lugged the boxes from his studio back to the Colony's main building, and set them on the porch there along with his suitcase, they decided to skip breakfast in the dining room and go into town instead, to have their breakfast in a proper restaurant. Neither said what Gad was sure that Hannah must be thinking, as he was—that their first meal alone was their last meal together.

Afterwards she stood with him on the porch to wait for his taxi. Her cheeks and her nose were very red, for overnight it had turned cold again; the mud was beginning to refreeze on the ground. He sang a line of the song they had written together and joked, feebly, "Not yet spring after all. Maybe we ought to revise it right now, quickly: 'Spring came and went in only a few days in these woods.'"

She smiled, but it was the sort of brave, doleful smile that made her look more forlorn than she had before he'd spoken, and he was sorry that he had. She'd been quiet all morning. She hadn't even said that she would miss him, or that she was sorry he was leaving. He knew that this was wise, and just right—and (for once, he thought) he'd been wise too, following her lead. If only she didn't look so sad! If she were to be sad, then he had to be too, and guilty as well. Wasn't it his fault if she was sad?

He thought about how what had drawn him to her from the first had been her happiness. A thought formed indistinctly in his mind then: if what had begun this—the "this" itself was indistinct—had been the very thing that he himself had taken from her, what had been the point of any of it?

He shut his eyes, briefly. He could not bear to look at her if she were to look so unhappy.

"Here's your cab," she said, and he looked. There it was, rounding the drive. He remembered looking out the window of the cab that had brought him here six weeks ago, turning off the road at the Colony's discreet sign, coming round this steep drive, wishing that the driver would stop talking— Gad had already heard too much about the famous artists he had driven to and from the Colony, and about "how lucky" he was to be coming here. He hoped he would not have the same cab driver. He hoped this one would not talk.

He shaded his eyes as the cab pulled up. He didn't look at Hannah but he said, "So you'll be. . ."

"All right? Of course." She managed a laugh. "Of *course*."

"Well, then. You take care of yourself, Hannah."

"Sure. You too."

For the first time, it bothered him that she never called him by name. She could have come up with something, he told himself. By now she could have. Dimly he was aware that he was trumping up a reason to be angry with her. Not too angry—just enough to get himself from where he stood into the backseat of the cab.

The driver, not the same one he'd had before, was coming up the steps to help him with the boxes and the suitcase.

"This all you've got?" he asked Gad, who nodded, fighting off the reflex to say, "Why? Should there be more?"

He glanced at Hannah. She still looked miserable, but she had her hands in the hip pockets of the puffy sky blue jacket she'd had to fish out again as the temperature dropped, and her eyes were on the mountains that poked up beyond the trees. She would marry Saint John, Gad thought, despite the doubts she had about him—doubts which she had never again voiced, perhaps never again *had*. And who was he to say she shouldn't?

"I'll get this," he told the driver; he picked up his suitcase. He didn't dare kiss her out here—who knew who might be watching? "Well, that's it, then," he said. Hannah nodded. She didn't take her hands out of her pockets.

That's it, then. He repeated this to himself as he waved, as the cab started down the drive. Hannah stood watching, and he could see her letting go of the effort she'd been making. It was possible that she was crying. He thought about how, long ago, Janet had loved him most when he was most unhappy. Or so it had seemed—and later she'd confessed as much when she announced that she'd begun "at last" to find his guilt and sorrow tiresome. For years, however, each time he came to the end of one of his amorous adventures, too wretched even to conceal his wretchedness from her, she would briefly become both more ardent and much kinder toward him. Later she described it as the "irresistible appeal of self-hate"; he had never been able to judge the extent to which this explanation was sarcastic. He couldn't see it, himself. Perhaps remorse and grief were appealing only to Janet. Or only to women. If so, it occurred to him as the cab picked up speed along the mountain road, perhaps that was the central trouble with Hannah's Saint John—that he never had anything to regret.

At home, he was surprised by Janet's mildness toward him. That he'd been so poor a correspondent, which he had assumed would cause him trouble, hadn't bothered her, she told him as they drove home from the airport. "I took it as a good sign. I figured it just meant that you were working hard." "I was," he said, humbled. And when she went on, "Plus, I figured that for once you'd taken my advice, and that as a result you'd actually made a couple of friends to occupy yourself with when you *weren't* working," he found that instead of being irritated (leave it to Janet to take credit if he'd had fun— the sort of thing that ordinarily drove him crazy), he was moved. "I did, in fact," he told her, looking out the passenger's side window at what Midwesterners considered slums: rows of tiny, over-brightly painted houses, each with its square of fenced-in yard and a scattering of toys and baby strollers. A man sat on the porch steps of a green-and-pink house; on one corner, a group of girls, none over nine or ten years old, stood talking urgently; a woman tugged the hand of a small, resistant boy—otherwise, the streets were deserted. "Where is everyone?" he said. "Where's who?" Gad turned from his window to his wife. "No one," he said. Then he added, "Thanks."

"For what? Picking you up at the airport? Letting you go in the first place?" She glanced at him. "My good advice?" She laughed. "No charge."

He hadn't been aware of the extent to which he'd girded himself for battle. It took the better part of a week before he ceased to say a silent prayer of thanks for every kindness—or, more to the point, he understood after the first few days, every absence of unkindness. This carried him along for days. When he played the sinfonietta and the concerto for her, and she said, "Nice. So it was productive. Good," his relief and gratitude (no sarcasm, no criticism! For once, no malevolence of any sort) were such that for the first time in his recollection he did not feel hurt or disappointed by her lack of enthusiasm.

He thought of Hannah; naturally, he did. But he did not expect to hear from her. They'd made no plans to keep in touch—on the contrary, it was understood that they wouldn't. They hadn't even traded their phone numbers or addresses. All she knew was the name of the city where he lived and the name of the university that kept him and Janet there; all he knew was which street she lived on in the Village, and that her building (crumbling red brick, just three stories high—she had described it in a poem she'd written at the Colony, one she'd called "Hat, Heart, Hearth") was one building (taller, light gray, with a storefront on the ground floor) removed from a corner—he didn't even know which corner! They could not have called or written to each other if they'd wanted to. At least— he checked the calendar that Janet kept on a nail on the wall by the kitchen phone—not once the next five days passed, and she had disappeared into her own life.

It was inevitable that he'd sometimes think of things he wished he could say to her—inevitable, he told himself, that he'd sometimes feel lonely: he'd grown so used to her company and her conversation. And wasn't it inevitable, too, he was obliged to ask himself, that when he made love to Janet he would sometimes think of Hannah? Certainly it was, but it would pass—this he knew from his past experience. Still, after it had happened twice (his first night at home, and once again, on his tenth night) he was sufficiently unnerved—the images of Hannah slipping out of jeans and flannel shirt and rolling toward him, her hair spilling over both of them, had visited him so persuasively he had been shaken: it was as if the spectral Hannah who had once looked in on him at work without his knowledge had purposefully dropped in on him here and lay down between him and his wife—he now made sure Janet was asleep before he came to bed (it wasn't as if their not making love was a great deprivation for either of them, he reasoned: for years he'd felt—and she had more than once confirmed, in terms that had appalled him—that sex with him, for her, was a responsibility, an obligation she felt bound to honor, "resulting in comparatively little pleasure in view of the effort expended"). She didn't mention the change, and so he didn't either. If she'd asked, he would have told her he was working late—he was in the middle of something. This would have been an outright lie, for he had not been able to work at all since coming home (but—this he told himself wryly—he did seem to be in the middle of *something*).

It was impossible for him to work. What he had written during his last week at the Colony made no sense to him here, and while he could remember thinking that the bits and pieces of his "ode" were distinct and even contradictory and yet mysteriously linked, he could not remember why he'd thought so, or what he could possibly have meant by this. He played the fragments again and again, but he could not begin to guess why he had ever had the idea they meant anything at all or were in any way related to each other.

Hannah lingered in his mind in an unpleasant, even irritating way. He was reminded of the way a bad cold hung on, weeks after the worst of it was over, with the remnant of a cough or a dull, chronic headache. He told himself that patience was required, that he'd fallen out of his old habits and thus had forgotten how to extricate himself as easily as he once had. Then he was ashamed of having thought this was about her. She had been his friend—his first new friend in more than twenty years. If they *hadn't* slept together, they would still be friends. By now he would have written to her, called her on the payphone at the Colony. Or she might have called him, on impulse, while she waited for the dinner bell to ring, to ask him how he was adjusting to "real life." *Then* Janet would have been suspicious, he thought. Oddly enough, it was having slept with Hannah that made it easier to resume ordinary life at home—"ordinary life" with the marked improvement of this new civility between him and Janet.

But was it really an improvement? True, it was exactly what he'd wished for from her, for too many years to count. How often had their worst (and stupidest—they always fought the hardest over things least worth the battle) fights wound down with his telling her that while he no longer hoped for kindness, much less love, it was beyond him why she couldn't manage simply to be civil to him? "Civility is impossible under the circumstances," she would tell him coldly.

Had the circumstances changed? Was she going to spring something on him? Did she *know* something—was she biding her time before she made an accusation? As the day of Hannah's departure from the Colony came and went (and with it his last chance of contacting her, short of turning up in New York and strolling down her street hoping he'd recognize the building from the poem—calling her name? casting his eyes upward for a glance of her framed in a third-floor window? He mocked himself; he thought, *Who needs Janet's sarcasm when I can make myself feel like an idiot at least as well as she used to?*), he turned watchful and suspicious.

Then one night at dinner, when she asked him how he'd liked the salad she had made, and he did not say—though it would have been the truth—that he hadn't noticed (that, indeed, although only a minute had passed since he'd taken his last bite, he could not remember having eaten it, he'd done so with such scant attention, interest, or pleasure), but instead said, "Lovely! Just delicious, Janet, thank you," and *she* smiled and said, "You're welcome," he thought (at first, idly), *How much easier it is to be polite. How is it that I never knew?* —and then he understood that if she wasn't "like herself" it was because *he* had changed toward her, that she was different because he was. And it was not only that he had become polite to her, or that since his homecoming (for once!) he had done nothing to antagonize or bait her, it was also that he wasn't *trying* to be nice—for she would have pounced on that: she would have seen it as a cover-up for something. He wasn't trying to be or to do anything, he was just going about his business. He wanted to be left alone—he didn't want to fight, or to be criticized or mocked; he didn't want to be required to defend himself—and he had stumbled on the way to be assured of that.

He had stumbled on *all* the ways to be assured of that. He saw it now. Since the moment he'd returned, he had done everything she'd asked of him without complaint or even question. And why not? Nothing she demanded of him was the least bit difficult. Cut the grass, take out the trash, sit here and listen to me while I complain about this or that. How was it he had never known before what he should do when she complained? For here was something else he'd blindly stumbled upon: simply listening without saying a word until she finished, then making a sympathetic, wordless noise. How little effort this required! How much less than trying to come up with some feeble, entirely useless (so she'd always say) suggestion about how to fix the problem! All he had to do now was to look compassionate and grunt and click his tongue— evidently all she'd ever wanted.

And he had discovered this not only without making any effort, but *because* he'd ceased to make an effort, because—

the realization stopped him dead, and he had to set down both fork and water glass so that he could rest both hands palms down on the table, steadying himself—he'd ceased to care. He'd ceased to care about Janet and his marriage, about making things right between them (as if he ever could have!). At this late date he was able to treat Janet as she wanted to be treated only because he no longer cared about how he was treated *by* her. Thus—O, irony!—at last she had ceased to treat him unkindly. Now that he'd lost interest in trying to persuade her to *be* kind, she had softened toward him.

This revelation might have depressed him had he not already been so overcome by lassitude. As it was, he felt relieved—utterly convinced—that there was no storm waiting to erupt on the horizon. He and Janet continued to exchange pleasantries and he continued to accomplish nothing, no longer even trying to work. He had put away the piece he'd started during his last week at the Colony and he had not thought about beginning something else. He did what had to be done, and when every chore, of Janet's devising and of his work's necessity—phone calls, letters, sending out the manuscript of his concerto—was done, he went into his room and closed the door and sat at the piano gazing out the window or lay on the battered vinyl couch that was a remnant from their first apartment (a Salvation Army find back then, which Janet had let him have when they'd bought a new, "proper" couch for the house, years ago) and read or listened to music. He found himself listening to the tapes he'd played for Hannah and to old records they had talked about, music they both liked but had never had the chance to listen to together: Blind Faith, Laura Nyro, The Band, Sandy Denny.

Summer began. He tried to rouse himself to prepare for the course he had agreed to teach fall quarter—sorry now that he'd said he would do it, although at the time, just before he'd left for the Colony, he'd had the idea that being asked was something of an honor. He'd taught Music Theory I at

least a dozen times over the years (that, and Great Master-
pieces of Music for Non-majors were the lecturer's staples);
this was his first chance to teach Theory II, and he'd been
told that by the time prospective majors took this course, the
less gifted, less serious and less "motivated" ones had been
weeded out. Three months ago this had appealed to him;
now the thought of trying to make "harmony, part-writing,
analysis and creative application"—such was the course description he'd been given by the Department's secretary—
clear and interesting to a bunch of nineteen- and twenty-year-
old Middle Western kids, half of whom would be named Dave
or Matt (the girls would be Jennifer and Heather), most of
whom would stumble to the morning class hungover from
the night before's frat party, wearied him so thoroughly he'd
fall asleep whenever he tried working on the syllabus. He'd
start out at the little table he used as a desk, sitting in the
straight-backed wooden chair, legal pad and pen and coffee
cup before him, and he'd last perhaps five minutes before
drifting over to the couch with its cracks and splits mended
with plastic tape that almost matched the saddle-colored vinyl. He thought of the pleasure Hannah took in preparing
even the most elementary of the courses she taught ("Poetry:
Read it and Write It!" was the one she would be teaching at
the Y this summer; in the fall she had two courses, he knew,
at The New School: "Becoming a Poet [or Just Learning to
Think Like One]" and "Journals and Dream Diaries: Tapping
into the Roots of Poetry"), but instead of inspiring him this
made matters worse, for reminding himself that she was teaching at the Y right now led to frequent assaults of images of
her in the classroom—where she was perhaps at this very moment, he would think as he lay, enervated, on the couch (which
hadn't had this much use, he reflected, even when it had been
in the living room of their first apartment). He saw her sitting
on the edge of a desk, pushing her hair back from her face
with one graceful, beringed hand, making clever jokes her

students laughed at appreciatively without pausing in their note-taking.

He was still waiting to stop thinking about her. But summer ground on and nothing changed, except perhaps for the worse. He accomplished nothing. He felt tired and jumpy at the same time. Too often, as he lay on the couch, which had begun to spring new cracks he didn't trouble to tape over, he went over bits of their conversations in his mind. He thought of the afternoon she'd told him what was wrong with "nearly all contemporary poetry. Either it's unbeautiful, as if language itself didn't matter—as if there could be poetry without beauty!"—and he recalled how she had pushed her hair back from her face and let her hand rest on her forehead, fingers buried in her black hair, so that the rings she wore turned for a moment into a small glittering tiara, her back resting on the cot they would move up to in another moment—"or else it's *only* beautiful, and then it's empty, meaningless. It doesn't connect to anything outside itself." He remembered the way she'd looked when he'd answered, taking in his own the hand she'd extricated from her hair, "Yes, the same is true in music today, too. You'd think people had forgotten that it's the relationships among notes that make a piece of music meaningful—that without tonality, there's no beauty. And when I do find beauty, it's without emotion, as if the two were contradictory. What sense is there in that?" How she had smiled at him then!

He remembered ranting to her one day that to his mind things had been on their way downhill "since the Renaissance"—that before that, art had had a daily role in people's lives, before the artist's personality took over, "before it mattered, say, *who* made the paintings in the churches, before it became all ego" (he could no longer remember what had provoked this diatribe; it must have been something he'd overheard at breakfast, or a flyer in their mailboxes about a presentation to be made that evening). Too much of art now spoke to no one but the artist and perhaps three of his fellow practitioners, he'd declared, and Hannah had leapt up from the floor and said, "Oh, yes! That's true, exactly!"

He imagined himself making the same speech to Janet, imagined her rolling her eyes and calling him—albeit in the mildest and most courteous of tones—a crank and a reactionary. And then with a smirk allowing that he was of course quite right about one thing: that the artist of today was nothing but a runaway ego train on a one-man track.

But he had ceased to speak to Janet except about the most trivial things. It was now unimaginable that he would attempt to have such a conversation with her. He thought with distaste of his efforts (so raucous, so reckless, so *vulgar*) over the years to attain her attention, her concern, her esteem. Her love.

She didn't seem to mind that he'd ceased to require her attention, or that since those two unhappy, early efforts, he'd avoided making love to her. Either she hadn't noticed or she was glad to be done with it—he had no way of knowing; they didn't talk about it. They had stopped talking altogether, really, except for the most purely banal of exchanges— regarding meals and chores and errands—and all was peaceful between them. Even when she complained about him (which, though she had less cause to do now than she had ever had before, she still occasionally did—in a reflexive, absent-minded, almost gentle way, as if she felt she had to keep her hand in: "Oh, don't tell me you forgot to put gas in the car *again*," or, "I see you missed recycling day. More important things on your mind, I suppose, than bringing the bin out to the curb?"), he would bow his head and register no protest or defense.

He would not have called himself depressed; he would not even have called himself unhappy (but in any case, he spoke to no one about how he felt, so there was nobody to whom he might have called himself anything). He had no interest in defining his condition. He was waiting something out—that was as far as he went in explaining himself to himself.

While he waited, he did nothing—almost nothing. Often, when he was certain Janet was asleep, and sometimes even in the daytime when he heard her leave the house, he'd go into the living room and rummage through the bookshelves, or steal into her study and examine the books there, looking for the names of poets Hannah had mentioned or quoted from to him. He'd read hurriedly—too hurriedly for real comprehension—afraid of being caught, even in the middle of the night. Afraid of looking foolish? Of Janet's mockery? Of having to admit to something he himself did not understand? He couldn't say. He preferred not to think about it.

Just wait, he told himself. Just wait and it will pass. But he told himself this with dwindling conviction, for summer was nearly over. It seemed to him now that his not calling Hannah when he'd had the chance, before she'd left the Colony, showed admirable strength—it showed both restraint and moral rectitude. Perhaps not up to Saint John's, he thought (he even managed a mordant laugh as he lay on his couch on a late August afternoon and toyed with the puffy off-white stuffing that was debouching from cracks all around him, the cushion lumpy with the two volumes of poetry he'd slipped beneath it when he'd heard Janet come in from wherever she'd just been)—he was no saint, he told himself. Still, it was something, he thought; it meant something.

But on another day he told himself: *Fool, how could you not have called her while you could!* Even if only to apologize! Guiltily he thought of how she'd looked the day he'd left. She had been his friend—how good she had been to him!—and he had done her harm. He'd undermined her future; he had made her sad and worried. *He* had given her cause for guilt.

And yet he knew it wasn't likely that she'd think of it that way. She thought more highly of him than she should. She would not blame him.

Once more—with considerably less self-mocking coolness—he imagined himself going to New York, wandering along her street hoping to spot her building. And now, for the first time, he thought too about writing to her in care of the Colony and asking to have the letter forwarded. But then if she (*if* she!) wrote back and Janet happened to pick up that day's mail before he did, how would he explain who Hannah Sampas was? She'd ask—no matter how much things had changed between them, she would ask. Or she would not *say* anything, but would hand over the envelope with a shrewd, suspicious look, one eyebrow up (he knew that look; he hated it). What would he say? "Oh, that's just someone I met at the Colony—you remember, I must have mentioned her." He saw the derision in her face, and the hostility; the dawning understanding and the accusations that would follow; himself fending them off; the two of them angry, bickering once more—and this made him so weary he rolled over on the couch and buried his face in the lumpy, sticky vinyl cushion.

Besides, what if he wrote to Hannah and she *didn't* write back? Think how that would make him feel.

He groaned into the cushion. For the first time, it occurred to him that he needed to talk. But to whom? He thought of each of his three closest friends: why could he not choose one of them and make a full confession—ask for help, advice? But his mind rebelled. And why? Because after so many years they were all Janet's friends as well as his? But this was not convincing. This had never stopped him in the past from talking to them—to all three of them, in long, late-night conversations—about his past romances. And they had encouraged him in this, admitting jocularly that they (faithful husbands all) enjoyed the vicarious thrill of his adultery. And yet he'd talked to all of them since his return and he had never once been tempted to speak Hannah's name.

He was up from the couch and pacing. He could not

speak of her, not the way he'd spoken, in the past, of others. He could not explain her to *himself*—his condition now was insupportable—so how could he explain her, or the state that he was in, to anyone?

That Hannah could not be admitted to the omnium-gatherum of all the other women he'd felt free to speak of to his friends—to confess his fleeting, trumped-up love and then, weeks later, to worry out loud (at length, elaborately, exquisitely, and most likely entertainingly) about how to extricate himself from them—was itself a message, he knew: a message he should have deciphered when that jumble of memories he'd watched spill out, shaken loose by his and Hannah's first embrace, would not accommodate her. And the thought of that night in his cabin—the memory of what had passed between them, and of her distress and his despicable, unforgivable behavior afterward—left him feeling faint. Before he could take steps (what steps? he asked himself viciously) to prevent it, he had begun to weep as pitifully as she had then.

What now? he thought. *What now?*

As the days crept forward toward the start of the new academic year, indistinguishable from one another, he felt himself sinking—drowning. He never knew what day it was, and sometimes as he lay on his couch he would fail to notice that day had lapped over into night. Janet was busy with meetings, rushing here and there. She was often gone now even for meals, which was just as well; he had all but given up eating. He managed to work up a meager syllabus for his course, sitting at his desk for ten or fifteen minutes at a time until he had arrived at something minimally usable. After he had driven down to campus with it, photocopied it and left the copies in his own temporary mailbox in the Music Department, he went home and slept for two hours, as if he had just spent the afternoon loading cement bricks onto a truck.

How, he wondered, would he propel himself to campus, teach a course for two hours twice a week, grade student work—be interesting in a classroom? How would he stay up-right and awake?

Janet seemed not to be aware of his torpor or his mis-ery. The old Janet, he thought as he lay on the couch one morn-ing, listening to the sounds of her bustling about in the other rooms, getting ready to go somewhere (to her office? to a meet-ing? a lunch date? the pool?—for she seemed to have taken up swimming again, twenty-five years after she had quit), the old Janet would have said, "I see that your artists' colony did you a world of good! How hard you've been working since you got home!" and handed him a roll of brown plastic mending tape: "a gift to help you in your work." But this Janet hadn't noticed the new cracks in the couch—she seemed not to have noticed that he'd *taken* to the couch. Or she had noticed but she didn't care.

She didn't mind, she said, that he had begged out of the social functions that marked the start of the new year—"Oh, they've never been much fun for you, I know," she said with breezy affability (and he didn't have the will to point out that she had discounted this for years, insisting that the only reason he would try to "weasel out" of these occasions was to irritate her)—but for one, a gala brunch he was *required* to at-tend with her, she told him, as it was impossible for her to go alone and she enjoyed this party too much every year (a couples-only, dress-up function, complete with a string quar-tet and caviar on toast points served by female students in maids' uniforms) to sacrifice it for the sake of his—she smiled in her new way, a TV newscaster across the breakfast table, all bad news and geniality—"agoraphobia."

Unfortunately, this was the event Gad hated most. It was given annually on the Sunday afternoon before fall quarter courses started, by a Comp Studies professor whose wife had family money (derived, it was said, from the ownership of coal mines), in a house and garden that came as close to being an estate as was possible in this part of the country. Couples with-

out children—and couples who could be depended on to leave
such children as they had at home with sitters—stood about
the lawn and in the house's numerous ground-floor rooms, all
the men in suits and all the women in the sort of dresses they
had no call to wear in this town except at this one party, even
Janet at this one event in spiky high heels and eye makeup
("It's like a costume party," she had more than once over the
years explained to him with exaggerated patience). He had
been told by the hostess years ago—he'd never known for sure
if she'd been serious—that single people were excluded by the
same logic that excluded children: "This is a party for
grownups." Grownups from throughout the University were
present, with their spouses, as were grownups of the wife's
acquaintance—the women of her reading group, the other
members of the various Boards of Directors on which she
served—with *their* spouses, all of whom were either lawyers,
politicians (for the town was the state capital), or executives of
the large corporation that was one of three significant employ-
ers in town (along with the University and state politics).

This year the party seemed particularly ludicrous, os-
tentatious, coarse, and idiotic to him, though he could not decide what bothered him most: the stultifying conversation
among businessmen and lawyers he heard all around him, the
false heartiness of the midwestern politicians, the academic
dreariness of Janet's colleagues ill-disguised by party clothes
(and still one could pick them out so easily from the non-aca-
demics! They *looked*, Gad thought, as if they were wearing
costumes, and he whiled away some of the slowly passing time
trying to determine why exactly this was), the self-conscious
efforts at political correctness evidenced by representatives of
as many racial minorities as could be located among the fac-
ulty and at the Statehouse (the corporation, it seemed, offered
none to choose from), and the same-gender couples in modest
but noticeable numbers, or the condescension with which he
was treated by all, since he fit in nowhere.

As he did every year, he drank too many mimosas. But this year he didn't eat, and so he got much drunker, faster. And although in past years at this awful party he had mingled, as per Janet's orders, involving himself in conversation after conversation that went nowhere and left him feeling vaguely humiliated—by the assumption (of the representatives of the Academy) that because he wasn't one of them he was a failure, the implication (by the representatives of Business) that he was some sort of highbrow phony, and the conclusion (by just about everyone else) that his work was nothing more than an excuse for not having a job—this year he hid out and talked to no one.

This protected him for the first hour, during which he plucked a total of four champagne flutes from passing silver trays (and lost sight of Janet, last seen chatting with a tall, blond, smiling man he guessed to be a state senator). He then began to keep himself amused, as far as that was possible, by trying to match party guests with occupations. College professors were easy, of course (though he made it harder, venturing to give them each departments, fields, and ranks), as were politicians; it was only when he tried to differentiate among the rich-by-birth, attorneys, and executives of one branch or another of the corporation that he had to use his brain. He was studying a slim, ferociously tanned woman in a short black dress and glossy black hair pulled back from her forehead so aggressively her outlined eyes bugged out, and having come to the conclusion that she was too serious- and nervous-looking to be a moneyed wife and too tensely elegant to be a lawyer, trying to determine if she was a vice-president in the women's clothes division (youth-oriented, more mature/career, or larger sizes?—he'd learned the sub-branches in a dismal conversation in this very room some years ago), the bath products line, or the chain of mildly risqué lingerie stores, when someone sought *him* out. "You're scowling," said the fellow as he joined him in his corner next to an enormous silver urn brimming with gladiolas. "Nice party." The two lines, taken together, made no sense to Gad, and he turned to consider the intruder, who immediately introduced himself at length. He'd had too much champagne too, Gad surmised. That he was legal counsel for the corporation *and* taught at the Law School complicated the game Gad had been playing, and so he felt justified, when asked to identify himself, in saying that he was a professor of fashion design, heir to a large family fortune, and a frequent consultant to the head of the corporation. The lawyer nodded; he was too drunk to be skeptical.

And all at once—Gad could not for the life of him have said why—he found himself telling this drunk, balding, temporarily and artificially credulous lawyer about a lawyer he knew in New York, a real do-gooder, practically a saint, who was betrothed to the most fascinating woman, a quite good poet and an otherwise extraordinary person. The lawyer listened closely, it seemed to Gad, and then, when he paused for a breath—in fact Gad felt as if he needed air, and as if air was the substance he was least likely to be able to attain just now, or that such air as there might be here was not likely to be usable—said, "Have you tried the smoked salmon? With cream cheese and capers? They were bringing it around no more than half an hour ago. I think I'll try to find some more before it's gone." And then he lumbered off, first bumping into the tall silver urn beside him, so that it tipped dangerously and Gad had to make a grab for it himself to right it. Gladiolas brushed his face and he felt his eyes fill with tears. He was wasting his life, he thought.

Janet appeared then, and grasped his elbow, pulling him along with her. He expected her to scold him—to disgrace him—but instead she steered him to a couple (elderly, but handsome; they might have been retired academics, both of them, or representatives of genteel old money—the old man was even dignified-looking enough to be a deposed state politician), introduced him by his full name and profession, without adding that he was her husband, and then vanished. The tall, silver-haired old woman asked him what he thought of the local orchestra—"I have to admit that I often find myself wishing it were more accomplished," she confessed before she had allowed him to respond, and her husband put in, quickly, "For a fellow like yourself, it's probably a bit small-time, no?" and asked him what he was working on just now. He was undone by this question. He excused himself, found Janet— she was laughing, talking with two other women dressed to kill, in high heels and short dresses—and told her he was leaving; no, he didn't want the car keys; he would walk.

On the two-miles-plus walk home and for the remainder of the day, during the restive night that followed, and the morning after, when he groped his way across the bedroom in the dark—an hour yet till daybreak, Janet snoring quietly on her side of the bed—he was sick at heart, filled with despair. The hopelessness and grief that had been gathering in him now seemed fixed and incurable, and as he paced from room to room and up and down the unlit stairs at six AM he contemplated living through the rest of his life in this state—sick of everything; disgusted with his life, with the senselessness and boredom of his days; without desire to go anywhere or do anything; without the possibility of happiness.

Janet, when he told her, after she had showered and had her first cup of coffee, that he needed to go to New York, was perplexed but unalarmed. She poured milk into her second cup of coffee and said, without looking at him, "Why? For how long? The quarter starts on Wednesday—you know I start teaching first thing that day. I have a nine AM. And don't you have class on Thursday afternoon?"

Of all the questions she had asked, he chose the second. "Just for a few days."

"But when would we go?" she said. He was following her now, from the kitchen to the living room, as she walked with her coffee cup and gathered what she needed for the day.

"I couldn't even manage a long weekend till fall quarter is over. I have meetings every Friday afternoon and classes first thing Monday mornings."

"Alone, I meant," he said. "Today. Maybe tomorrow. I haven't called the airline yet." And quickly: "I don't have to be on campus until Thursday afternoon at three. I can manage a quick trip."

She stopped moving, her hand in the large purse into which she had just stuffed a file folder and a paperback book. She looked at him, her eyes narrowed. His courage failing, as he'd known it would even when it had first come to him with the sunlight that had just begun to creep around the edges of the window shades of his own room, where he had settled himself finally at seven, he heard himself extemporize, "To see Doolittle. It's been too long. And he's been. . .he's been in bad shape. You know, since Cornelia filed for the divorce."

"No, I didn't know," Janet said, but he heard the hesitancy in her voice.

"Oh, yes, he's having a terrible time. Terrible."

The truth, he realized as he made this assurance, was that he had no idea how Doolittle was coping or not coping with his wife's having left him. He had announced it, as he had announced the filing of the papers some months later, without adding a word about how he was feeling (unless bitter, witty jokes were to be counted—and, if so, Gad didn't know *how* he was supposed to count them, as evidence of what). He had assumed, of course, that when Cornelia had first left, Doolittle had felt too humiliated, angry, and depressed to talk about it, and that it would have been rude to press the issue. But months had passed, and neither one of them had brought it up. But Janet was so easily convinced—"Well, then," she said briskly, as she turned from him and left the room, "certainly you should go. Poor Patrick!"—that he was left wondering not only if what he'd said could be true but how it could be that he didn't know.

Was there anyone, he asked himself, watching Janet return with her swimsuit and goggles and tuck them into her bag, about whom he knew anything of any real importance? Who knew anything of him? Only Hannah, he thought—only Hannah.

And he fled.

He took a cab from La Guardia into the Village. "Here," he told the driver at the easternmost end of the street she'd named. He had to force himself to walk, not run. He did not call her name, but he looked this way and that, searching for red brick, his eyes turned upward toward the third floor of every building that he passed. He thought of every way he'd failed so far in his life.

He told himself that if he reached the river and had not yet spotted Hannah's building, he would know that he had simply failed to recognize it; he would turn back and walk the length of the street again. But then there it was—exactly as she had described it in her poetry. A small, noticeably lopsided, dark red building, with overflowing trash cans parked in front of it, bars on the ground-floor windows. The pale gray building, two floors taller, stood beside it. The corner just beyond, he noted, was Gay Street. She should have put that in the poem, he thought.

He stared up at the row of third-floor windows and the paint-flecked fire escape that stretched across them. He didn't know which of them might be hers. Her apartment might not even face the street, he realized; she hadn't said. Still he looked up, shading his eyes, as if he might be able to divine which window was hers, or as if he could will her to it. Then he saw, or thought he saw, a cat, almost as dark as the darkness around it, on the sill of one of the third-story windows. A second later it had disappeared—jumped off into the apartment? Or had he imagined it?

It didn't matter. He told himself this, though his heart was beating violently. In a moment he would find her bell;

he'd ring it. If she wasn't home, he'd sit on the stoop and wait. He could see her in his mind, coming up the street after an evening out, stopping in astonishment when she saw him. He would stand up then; he would rush toward her and tell her that he couldn't live without her.

Because he couldn't—he felt this to be true. As he stood looking up at what might be her window in the crumbling red brick tenement, a building that was older and more thoroughly neglected than even Hannah's sad, sweet, witty poem suggested, he was certain that although what he had done—leaving home, with nothing but an overnight bag at his side, and coming here, to her—was only the first step on what would be a difficult and complicated path, what lay ahead for him, for both of them, was something so essential to their lives it *would* be death to fail to recognize and to embrace it.

At that instant the window screen beyond which he had seen the dark shape of a cat was lifted. Hannah leaned out. She smiled down at him, brilliantly.

Their real lives, he thought. Their real *life*, together. A new and glorious life.

HOPE AMONG MEN

There are two men in this story. They have names, of course, but I mean to call them Misery and Heartache, because that's how I think of them, and that's how my protagonist—her name is Hope (her real name, not an alias)—thinks of them, too. Besides, these are the names (this is how storytellers sometimes talk) these characters have *earned*.

They are not the only men Hope has known. There have been some others—far too many others, I might venture to say, if I were the kind of annalist who felt free to pass judgment; I am not. Thus I will say only that there have *been* others: twenty-two, to be exact (although, of these, no more than five are men with whom it could be said that Hope had "serious" relationships, and of the seventeen remaining, perhaps slightly more than half are men with whom Hope's intimacy lasted less than a full week, and in a few such cases, even less than twenty-four hours). This story is concerned with Misery and Heartache because their roles in Hope's life have been the most pointedly dramatic, and I want to tell a story, for once, that *has* drama—a story in which things happen. Besides, a story, it's been said (so I've said myself, more times than I can count), to be a story, requires its protagonist to change as a result of what takes place in it—and Hope herself believes that Misery and Heartache changed her. I don't believe that it's my place to disagree.

There's one other matter I would like to get out of the way now: I want to say right at the outset that Hope's romances with Misery and Heartache are long over. I say this knowing that it violates one of the basic principles of modern storytelling *(do not anticipate the future)*, that by doing so I am destroying the illusion of presentness that, as narrator, it's my responsibility to provide and maintain for you.

Call me irresponsible.

(Call me unreliable.)

What I am *supposed* to do is act as if the outcome of the events I describe is unknown, so that you can pretend, too, and be surprised by the way things turn out—just as you're surprised in "real" life. And yet when was the last time you *were* surprised by your life? What if this Aristotelian idea of literature as an "intense imitation" of life is *better* served by violation of the keep-the-future-secret principle than by the application of it? (And never mind that Hope would swear that she expected nothing but the best from these relationships. She had to be a fool not to see, early on—exactly as we do—that they were doomed.)

But there's another reason I am telling you now how things come out in the end. I want to make it clear from *word one* that the story I'm about to tell is not a love story. You do not get to root for the heroine to wind up with the right man. There is no right man. There is only Hope. There's Hope at the beginning, and there's still Hope at the end—and in between, for several thousand words, there's Heartache and Misery.

And now, at last, we may begin.

❂

In the beginning, Hope is in New York. She lives in a tiny apartment—one room, a perfect square, with a kitchen "area" along the western wall, and a water closet in the northeast corner. The apartment smells of oil and fish and pork and garlic and cooked cabbage (it is above a Chinese takeout in the East Village) and turpentine and paint (for which no one but Hope can claim responsibility). By now—the moment when this story opens—Hope has been here for just over seven years. She moved in when she started graduate school, thinking that it would do for the two years (it was so cheap, after all; surely she could bear it for that long), but when she was finished with school she had no idea where to go: she didn't want to leave New York, and there was no place *in* the city that she could afford to move to—so she stayed where she was, and looked for work.

At first, she had a part-time job in a pet store; then, briefly, in a donut shop; then she worked as a "temp," doing "light typing" for lawyers and financial planners and investment bankers; then she was a waitress in a macrobiotic restaurant, where sometimes an entire evening passed without a single customer; and then, for six months, she worked in a bookstore that sold only murder mysteries, biographies, and cookbooks—categories of books in which Hope, who would read almost anything, had no interest at all.

Finally—two years had passed by then—through friends of friends of friends, she got a job she liked, although it was no better paying than the others: she was hired by the owner of a gallery in SoHo to work part-time and learn "everything," he promised her, about art restoration and repair.

By the time we come into her life, she has been working there for three years, all day every Monday, when the gallery is closed, and for the last year and a half she's had a second part-time job, two days a week, at an "alternative museum" in an outer borough, where she has a proper title: she is Director of the Department of Art Conservation, Restoration and Reparation. She is in fact the only person *in* the "department," and the pay, title or not, is just as low as it continues to be at the gallery, where by now all the restoration and repair is left to her (the truth is that there's very little restoration to be

done at either place; mainly what Hope does is make repairs
on damaged artwork). Still, she likes both of her jobs—she's
never bored by them, and there are times when the work gives
her real pleasure—and her schedule suits her well: it leaves
her four full days each week, and all her evenings, free for her
own work.

Hope's own work is painting; more specifically, the
painting of small, brilliantly colored landscapes. They come
out of her head and not from life—that is, they are entirely
imaginary landscapes—and because of this, and also because
they are never any bigger than six by eight inches, she can
paint as easily in the East Village as in Woodstock or
Stockbridge or somewhere in Maine or Montana (or so she
finds herself saying at parties, to people who have asked the
usual, annoying question about what her work is "like," and
who then say, "But then how can you live in the *city*?") or anywhere else, for that matter: *any* city, big or small, on either
coast—or mid-sized, in the middle of the country (which, as it
happens, comes in handy, when a little later in this story she
gets a job offer *in* a mid-sized city in the middle of the country). She doesn't need much space, and prefers not to be disturbed by light from the outside (she shuts the shades on her
two windows and turns on a clamp-on lamp that hangs above
her head when she is working), and therefore it wasn't hard
for her to set up on one side of the apartment after she had
finished school and no longer had a studio on campus. She
tries not to think about what five years (five years so *far*, she
tries not to tell herself) of living with the fumes produced by
her work might be doing to her—she keeps both small windows open, day and night, year round, and sleeps as distantly
as possible from where she works (she's measured it—the exact distance, bed to worktable: it's twelve feet, four and one-
half inches)—tries *hard* not to worry, because what choice does
she have? She can't stop painting and she can't afford to rent
a separate studio. She tries, too, without success, to keep from

worrying about her work—by which she means the paintings themselves, and the making of them—and about her "career" as an artist (the "public" aspect of the work—shows, grants, prizes, fellowships, awards—of which there has been very little, for Hope is not—or so she has been told by artist friends who are—sufficiently aggressive). She tries not to worry about what will happen *next*—tries not to think at all about the future. If she does, she ends up thinking that her life will stay exactly as it is forever: she will live forever in one room above the Chinese takeout, working on one side of it and sleeping, eating, reading on the other; never have a solo show; never earn more than nine thousand dollars in a year; and one day find that she has somehow turned into an eighty-year-old woman, a failed artist—old and poor and unknown and alone.

She tries not to worry about loneliness.

Tries not to—tries to tell herself that it will pass; or that it won't and she'll "get used to it": that she *should* be alone (an artist should); that surely she can't "need" a man to make her life complete; that loneliness will force her to grow stronger. That it's *only* loneliness, it's no big deal: she'll live. It seems to her that she should "rise above it"—and that she *can't* makes things worse, because along with feeling lonely she feels weak for being lonely.

For some time now, Hope has been depressed.

Once in a while she meets someone—through friends of friends, or friends of friends of friends, or in the neighborhood, or through one of her jobs—to whom she is mildly attracted (or at least by whom she is not repelled) and sometimes—rarely—that feeling is returned (or anyway acknowledged) and, just briefly, the problem seems "fixed." Later—afterwards—it's always embarrassing. The fact is: this is a bad stretch for Hope.

At last she comes to the conclusion that she should "get out more," meet new people—people who are *not* friends of her friends, or friends of friends of theirs, or who have busi-

ness in the gallery or who are making a delivery to the museum, or who are the nephew or ex-brother-in-law of someone who works with her in the museum or the gallery or
of someone who has passed through one of these two places,
or whom she will have to run into in the supermarket or the
hardware store for the rest of her life. She will have to make
an effort.

She decides to take a class.

It seems to her a bit cliché, this idea—which makes
Hope uneasy (for she hates the thought of turning into a
stereotype); she consoles herself by thinking that she probably
won't meet a soul who interests her. And really, she thinks,
she *ought* to be taking classes anyway, for reasons that are *not*
suspect. As an art student she never even thought of taking
non-required courses in the history of art—she wanted to spend
all her time, then, in the studio—but what she doesn't know
has begun preying on her, and it isn't such a bad move, she
thinks, to take a course or two now, to fill in some of the gaps
in her education.

Satisfied by her reasoning, she chooses an art history course (and then has to steel herself to ask permission
of the course's instructor before she can register for it—
which requires a considerable sacrifice of pride; this is followed by the realization of how great a sacrifice of painting
time she will be making—because although the seminar
meets only once a week, the sessions are each three hours
long, and with the time spent getting to the university and
back *and* the time she'll be spending in the art library, studying, the hours seem to stack up alarmingly; and then there
is the sacrifice she has to make financially to take the
course—which is the toughest, when it comes down to it, of
them all, since she has hardly any money to begin with. But
it turns out that she doesn't mind making these sacrifices—
that she's *pleased* that it's turned out to be more difficult to
manage this than she had guessed it would be. That there

are sacrifices to be made helps reassure her that she isn't doing something frivolous).

The seminar is in Northern Romanticism; eight of the ten students are working toward PhDs in art history. At first she is shy in class—there's so much offhand reference to critics and historians Hope's never heard of—but on the third week she surprises herself: during a discussion of the German, Scandinavian, and English visionary landscapes of the early nineteenth century, she is not only outspoken but passionate. She had no idea she had so many strong opinions about Caspar David Friedrich, and to hear herself defending him—defending, indeed, *all* of landscape painting—against what seem to her reductive "charges" of specific meaning and symbology, is both shocking and thrilling to her.

It is on that day, just as the class session ends—everyone rustling and shuffling, scraping back their chairs, hoisting Danish schoolbags and reclipping pens to shirtfront pockets, drifting forward to confer in low tones with the teacher—that the one other "outsider" in the group, a grad student in history (that's all Hope knows about him—that's how he introduced himself when they went round the room the first day), asks her if she has time for a cup of coffee. She's still flushed, excited by her nerviness; she says *sure, yeah, why not* to the coffee—she's preoccupied; her mind's on what she said in class; she's not even listening to herself respond to him—and then, when he suggests a Greek diner on Broadway, and just stands there, waiting for her, she comes to: she looks at him for the first time—looks at him *really*—and decides he's sort of cute in an extremely *bookish* way, and nods agreement to the diner, smiles, and asks him if he thinks that she offended anybody. *He* smiles, says no, they can take it; and as they leave the room together he says he admires her fervor; she says, "Is *that* what you call it?" and, as they proceed down the hall, down the stairs, out of the building and across the campus, he begins to ask her questions—lots of questions (good ones, too, she

thinks)—about her own work (she had described her*self*, that
first day, as a landscape painter, he reminds her—as if she needs
to be reminded, which strikes her as strange; but perhaps this
is a way of flirting, letting her know he remembers what she
said two weeks ago?).

Over coffee at the diner, he tells her about *his* work: he
is writing a doctoral dissertation about violations of the laws
of war versus the concept of a nation's sovereignty. He's taking the art history course for "the simple pleasure of it," he
says, and to give himself a little respite from the dissertation,
which he has been struggling with since finishing his
coursework "many years ago," he tells her with a sigh (although when pressed—because she can't help pressing, curious about how long the academic process takes—it comes out
that by "many" years he means two and a half—"so far," he
hastens to add). He chose *this* course, he says, because Romanticism, "if one is to define it as a movement celebrating
the supremacy of feeling over reason," is his "favorite all-time
art movement." Hope can't tell how seriously she's supposed
to take him, but she likes him—she thinks he is sweet. He's
like a grown-up boy more than a man, she thinks: a clever boy
who's showing off his cleverness, to charm her—and it's working, she *does* find him charming, if a bit ... self-dramatizing.

This, of course, is Heartache.

They talk for a long time that day, and then again the
next week too, when once again they go out after class for coffee. He tells her about Germany and Scandinavia, the Low
Countries and England in the nineteenth century, to give her a
"political, historical, and cultural context" for the art they're
looking at in this course; he demands to know what she thinks
"as an artist" about the strange light and the vast distances
depicted in so many of the landscapes painted in the earliest
part of the century—and asks if she doesn't agree that these
had a "direct and obvious effect" on later nineteenth century
American and European landscape painting; he speaks of Con-

stable, Cole, Van Gogh (he says "Go*ch*"), Cezanne, Gauguin, Courbet, and the Barbizon School—and he also speaks of literature, architecture, physics, current politics (about which she knows very little; Hope tends to stay out of politics), the Oil Crisis, the Great Depression, Preston Sturges movies, music (it emerges that he is an opera buff), t'ai chi, Thai food, Judaism—he has guessed that Hope is Jewish—World War II, isolationism, and Alaska (the Alaska Highway, in particular—he has just read a book about it).

Hope has a weakness for men who know things. Inevitably, then, she is susceptible to Heartache, and naturally she's drawn up short when he—as they are saying their goodbyes after their second conversation over coffee—mentions that he's married (he doesn't *mention* it; he simply uses the phrase "my wife and I." He says: "Alas—my wife and I are going out of town this weekend, when I'd sooner stay home and get some work done"). Hope is disappointed. But she takes it in stride—after all she hardly knows him. She writes him off as a romantic possibility, and remains pleased to have met him, and pleased too that they are going to be friends (for by now they are already on their way to *that*—well on their way. This much seems certain).

Later she will ask herself if she was lying to herself then; she'll decide that she was not, exactly—that perhaps she wasn't being "realistic," but that "lying" is undoubtedly too strong a word for what she did (which was to tell herself, as the weeks passed and their long talks over too many cups of coffee after class at the Greek diner turned into a weekly habit—*and* she found that she looked forward to the class each week excessively—that she'd developed something of "a crush" on him, but that there wasn't any more to it than that: that it was "just" a crush, and therefore innocent the way the crushes she had had at twelve had been, because she had no inclination to do anything about it and was quite content with "the way things were"; that is: content to keep her feelings to herself—

small feelings, anyway, she thought—and sit across from him
one afternoon a week and sip bad coffee as he careened wildly
from one subject to another. She felt, as she sat listening, that
she was learning things she'd never in a million years learn
otherwise. And if her pulse sped up unnaturally each Thursday as she walked into the classroom, *he* would never know; it
didn't matter).

    Looking back, she'll marvel over her naïveté. (I
shouldn't wonder if you don't, too.) But at the *time* it all
seems...harmless. Friendly. Indeed, the two of them become
good friends. They tell each other a great many of the usual
things: anecdotes about their gifted, troubled childhood selves
and tales of adolescent misadventures, memories that they are
not quite sure *are* memories so much as family apocrypha, the
"truth" about their own abilities and talents (less plentiful and
less dependable than "the rest of the world" knows), and one
or two especially humiliating long-kept secrets (as if they'd
been saving them up just for this exchange of confidences).
And yet about his marriage, Heartache (in these early days, I
should point out, Hope called him "Heart") is reticent; in fact,
he *never* speaks of it, or of his wife, except in passing, as in:
"My wife likes that Chinese restaurant; I don't." As time goes
by, Hope meets the wife, however (that's how she thinks of
her: "*the* wife"): all three of them—the wife, Heartache, and
Hope—go out to dinner (twice; once to a concert afterwards).
The wife is smart and pleasant and attractive, a perfectly nice
woman, a grad student in math who sings in an early music
group for fun. Hope likes her—not so well as she likes Heartache, she acknowledges in silence, but so what? she thinks.
It's just a case, common enough, where one "gets on with" but
is not destined to become "best friends with," a friend's spouse.

    Meanwhile, Hope and Heartache *are* becoming "best"
friends. In addition to their weekly meetings, they begin now
to talk on the phone—at first only occasionally; then more often—twice, three times a week; then so regularly that, by the

semester's end, they rarely go a day without a phone call, and there are days when they call each other more than once. He wants to take another course with Hope, and when she tells him that she can't, that it will be some time before she can save up the money to do this again, he is crestfallen: he says, "But we'll never see each other, then." She tells him he's being silly, that of course they will.

But he's right; they don't. In the six weeks after the course ends, although they talk on the phone daily, often for an hour or more, they see each other only once, and then they're not alone—the wife is with them. All three of them go to dinner (Indian) and then to a movie (the new Eric Rohmer). This outing is the wife's suggestion—so Heartache tells Hope—and somehow, in the many hours that they spend on the telephone, neither Hope nor Heartache seems able to introduce the subject of their meeting by *themselves* for dinner or a movie—or a drink, or coffee; anything—and it crosses Hope's mind that they are afraid to; but she tells herself *she's* being silly: they're just busy, both of them.

Then one afternoon—an hour or so after one of their long talks on the phone—Heartache turns up, without warning, in Hope's neighborhood: calls from the corner, says, "Hello, it's me—again. I'm at a payphone half a block away. I want to see you. May I come up, or will you come out?" Hope is beset by so strong a rush of drastically conflicting feelings she can't speak at first. She's overjoyed, scared, thrilled, uneasy, giddy, anxious, flattered, angry with him. Finally she tells him to stay put, she'll come downstairs.

They are both uncomfortable as they sit drinking take-out coffee on a stoop a few doors down from Hope's place. Neither of them speaks of their discomfort; Heartache doesn't explain why he wanted suddenly to see her; Hope doesn't confess that she feels ashamed and guilty without knowing why.

They spend no more than an hour together, and it is an awkward hour of efforts to make "normal" conversation—

Hope finds that she cannot remember what a "normal" conversation *is* between them, and he seems to be just as confused as she is; both of them begin to say things they don't finish (Hope says, "What were you…" and trails off; Heartache says, "I wanted…" and falls silent). Then he goes home, and she goes upstairs.

Now three days pass—Friday, Saturday, and Sunday— during which she doesn't hear from him. She tries to reach *him* twice—once Friday night, when no one answers, and once Sunday morning, when the wife answers and very coldly, Hope thinks (but perhaps it's only paranoia) tells her he's not there; she doesn't know when he'll be back; would Hope like to leave a message?

On Monday, fifteen minutes after she has opened up the gallery, before she has begun the day's work (she has just sat down with a bialy, a container of black coffee, and the *Times*)—Heartache appears. He pounds on the glass door, which Hope has locked behind her; in the back room she hears fists thumping the glass and jumps—spills her coffee on her *Times*, and on herself, and curses—rushes out to the front, sees him, wonders at the sight, unlocks the door again, and lets him in. Luckily she is alone; on some Mondays the owner of the gallery comes in—and how would she explain this? Heartache is wild-eyed; he looks as if he hasn't slept since she saw him on Thursday—he looks haggard, rumpled; he looks as if he is about to cry. Hope says, "What's wrong? Are you okay?" and he says no, he's not okay: he's going crazy, he's in love with her—what's he supposed to do?

Hope suddenly feels faint. She stares at him and for a moment she cannot say anything. He stares back: it is as if he's issuing a challenge. At last she speaks; she whispers, "Don't do this. Please. It's absurd—you're *married*."

"Oh, for god*sakes*, Hope," he says, "*I* know I'm married. Do you think you have to tell me that?"

"Obviously I do," she says.

"And if I weren't? What then? If I were free, would you—?"

"But you're not," Hope tells him. Coldly, firmly. Her manner surprises *her*.

"But what if I *were*?"

"You're not."

"But what—"

"I don't *know*," she says. "Maybe then it would be different. But there's no point in this. You're *not* free. You *are* married. So just...just..." Hope stops; she feels her heart slamming around as if it's looking for a way out. "Please," she says, "just go *away*."

And he does. And once again she doesn't hear from him for three days. She doesn't call him this time—how can she?—but she's panicked by the thought that she might *never* hear from him. She hadn't meant for that to happen. But what *had* she meant to happen when she'd asked him to "just go away"? she asks herself. What does she want to happen?

She knows she ought to try to figure out how she feels—but she can't bear to. She can't stand to think about it.

Then on Thursday night, late, Heartache calls her, from a payphone. He is on the corner of Saint Marks and Second. He has left his wife. He has told her that he is in love with Hope. "Now I *am* free," he says. "*Now* will you discuss this? You said, 'Maybe then it would be different.' Is it different?"

Later Hope will worry that she had done something terrible by saying that—that if she'd said, instead, "There's *no* chance: I don't love you and I never will," he never would have left his wife—that she'd encouraged him, and that *that* had been every bit as bad as having an "affair" with him would have been. But that night—and for months following that night—she is too dazed, too happy and too stunned by her happiness, to worry about anything. *Neither* of them worry about anything. For months, they both are so happy they can do nothing at all except *be* happy, beyond the few things they have no choice but to do: go to their jobs; collect the books and clothes from Heartache's old apartment; see a lawyer to arrange a legal separation from the wife; pack up Hope's things, sublet her place, and move to a bigger one, together—a loft (small and overpriced) on Lafayette Street. Neither of them can get any work done: all they want to do is talk and touch. On weekends they unplug the phone, and from Friday to Sunday nights they are together without interruption: they cook as a team and eat their meals in bed; they hold hands when they go out to buy the *Times* or shop for groceries; they take showers, twice a day, together (Hope even sits with him, on the closed lid of the toilet, while he shaves). And if Heartache leaves her, even for an hour, he returns with gifts—with chocolates, perfume, flowers, earrings; once he brings home a kaleidoscope, and once an antique silver hand mirror.

After six months they begin to calm down. This is disappointing to them. By comparison their life seems ordinary now, a little dull—but they declare themselves "grown up and sensible" and tell each other that they'd always known that "things could not go on forever" as they had been. (*Who could live that way?* they ask; and *Who would want to, after all?* The questions are rhetorical, and neither makes an effort to provide a list of candidates.) Still, they must take turns reassuring one another that their feelings haven't changed—that they have merely grown accustomed to "the plain fact" of each other and can therefore (as they *must*, they tell each other gravely) now resume their own established occupations. And soon they both are busy: life slides back to normal. Heartache writes his dissertation; Hope paints.

Normal worries now creep in. The small loft is really too expensive for them. Bills are overdue; they snap at each other, then apologize, over the spending habits they have brought to this relationship. Since Heartache is already working at three different jobs (besides his graduate assistantship, he teaches at two other colleges—Introduction to the Great Figures of Modern Europe at one; Western Civ, from 1600 to the Present, at another), after much discussion Hope applies for, and gets (to her own surprise—for despite Heartache's urging and support she had been sure she wasn't qualified), a good, full-time restoration job, at a big gallery on Fifty-seventh Street that shows only the work of dead or very old artists, where she not only will earn more than she'd have guessed she ever would—but where, after the first six months that she is on the job, the gallery will pay for courses in art history and restoration.

A new routine begins. Hope works five days a week; on her days off, and every night, she paints. Heartache teaches in the daytime, and at night he haunts the library; sometimes he is there writing till midnight. On weekends, he goes up to campus and spends half-days in the office he shares with three other graduate students, grading student papers and exams; then, sometimes until quite late, until two or three AM, he is at the computer center, typing up what he has written that week. He and Hope don't see much of each other; they're rarely home at the same time, except to sleep. And often even when they both *are* home—after he has come in, late—she is still absorbed in her work; when she hears him at the door, she calls out (heading him off before he comes over to the corner of the loft in which she works, and starts talking to her) that he should go ahead to bed, she'll meet him there "in just a bit." A flash of guilt accompanies this every time—guilt mixed with sadness. But she doesn't feel as if she has a choice: when he's around while she is working, he tends to hover over her and comment on what she is doing and ask irritating questions, like why she won't "at least try, or *think* about" starting with photographs of actual places. "I prefer to make things up," Hope tells him lightly. "I *know* that," he says. "My point is *why*? *Why* do all your landscapes have to come out of your head? Why are you being so close-minded about this?"

"I suppose I *am* close-minded," she says, and thinks: and close-*mouthed*, too. Because she *wants* to tell him that it isn't any of his business, and she doesn't.

Almost nine months have now passed since Heartache left his wife for Hope. They have started bickering. These little arguments concern little things—who makes the coffee, who makes more long distance phone calls, who should make the bed. She wants him to do more, she says: she's not his maid. He says, "Do more? Like what?" She says, dryly: "Pick one, any one: sweep, vacuum, dust, pick up the laundry, do the dishes, take the garbage out, make sure there's milk for coffee." He says she's trying to domesticate him—and he yells at her: if he'd wanted to be married, he says, he would have stayed married. She bursts into tears. "You're sorry that you left her, aren't you," she says—and he says, "Oh, God, no, of course not. I was speaking flippantly, I'm sorry." And he strokes her hair and kisses her and promises he *will* do more.

But he doesn't, and the argument picks up again after a week or so. She says *look, I don't want you to do it all, I just want to split the duties with you equally.* He says *it will all get done, why are you making such a big deal out of it?* She says *no, it* won't *get done unless I do it;* she points out that for the first six months they were together *nothing* got done. He says he misses that first six months, and she says, *yes, I do too, but that wasn't real life and this is.* He says he despises real life; this time *he* bursts into tears.

Soon it comes out that he isn't happy about the idea of her taking classes. "But you wanted me to," she reminds him, astonished. "I wanted you to take a class *with* me," he says, "and that was when we had no other chance to see each other. Now your taking classes means we won't *ever* get to see each other." Hope says, "Oh, that's silly," which infuriates him. "Is it?" he says. "Is it? When do *you* suppose we'll see each other if you're working full time, painting, *and* going to school?" Hope tells him that he's busy too; she can't see why he's acting as if everything's her fault. Heartache says not *everything* is her fault, but it's plain to him that she wants to spend as much time as possible away from him, and accuses her of being interested in meeting other men. Hope, astounded, ends up screaming at him that she's interested in taking classes for the sake of learning something—not to get picked up by any more men looking for a way out of unhappy marriages.

A year after he has left his wife—the same week Hope goes up to NYU to register for her first restoration class—Heartache's divorce comes through. He weeps about it—weeps for days, in fact. For two days Hope is gentle with him—how can she not be, when he's so unhappy? Finally, when on the third day he shows no signs of recovering, she asks him again if he is sorry that he left his wife, and again he tells her no—but then he pauses, and he adds that he's not sure, however, that he should have left for Hope.

Now things between them get much worse. When Hope asks him for anything—to make a late-night run for milk for coffee in the morning, or even for a kiss goodbye before they go their separate ways at nine AM—he bristles, protests. Frequently, he tells her she's excessively demanding. She suggests that *anything* she asks for feels like a demand to him, that maybe he's just selfish. He says *oh, great, that's what my* wife *used to say;* Hope says, *uh huh—well, maybe we're both* right.

And yet they don't fight *all* the time. There are still lulls, when everything seems fine—fine enough even for them to talk about their difficulties frankly, but still peacefully. Then they laugh and are affectionate and go to bed together and call what's been happening to them their *Who's Afraid of Virginia Woolf Period of Adjustment.* But even in the lulls there is an undercurrent that makes Hope uneasy. Heartache often quotes to her—as if he's joking—a Yiddish folk saying that Hope herself had taught him in their early days together: "Fun loyter hofnung vert men meshuge." *With hope alone you can go crazy.*

Hope is still with Heartache—literally *with* Heartache, in the Museum of Modern Art, on the first Saturday in months when both have the day free—when she meets Misery. She and Heartache are standing in front of the big Miro in the hallway on the second floor when Misery (of course, Hope doesn't know yet that it's Misery) taps Heartache on the shoulder and says, without inflection, "Hey, what's shakin'?"

Heartache turns and then he grins. He says, "Well, well, well—how about that? You son of a bitch. How long has it been?"

Misery and Heartache shake hands, pat each other's shoulders, express their amazement that the other also lives in New York. Hope is introduced to Misery and told that he and Heartache had been undergraduates together at the small, expensive college in New England about which Hope has heard many stories. They had come to know each other in a series of the special seminars for brilliant students for which the school is famous, and over lunch at the museum Hope sits silently and listens as they reminisce about the course in which they'd met: *Philosophy of Modern European History*, taught entirely in German. They go on at length, both during lunch and afterwards, as they walk through the galleries together, about each of their dissertations. Misery's is on Spinoza—this is all Hope understands about it as she half-listens to them (she, for one, is looking at the paintings as they make their way through the museum); she does, however, register with some amusement Misery's description of himself as an epistemologist. She makes a private, silent joke—tells herself that if she had fallen for Heartache because he "knew things," here's the man she ought to leave him for: one who *knows* things about knowing things.

But she doesn't leave Heartache for Misery. It's Heartache who leaves her, not long after the afternoon at MOMA; he leaves her every bit as suddenly as he had left his wife—announcing one night when he comes home that he's sorry, but he thinks he made a bad mistake: he doesn't love her, at least not enough—"not enough to struggle through this and try making it work out," he says. He cries. He says, "I don't know, maybe I did love you and just stopped." He says, "Oh, Hope, I'm so unhappy I can't bear it." He actually (and she has never seen this done before—she's only read about it) beats his chest.

It is nearly a month later that Hope hears from Misery. He calls and tells her that Heartache had called *him*, just the night before, for the first time since running into him at the museum—that he'd called looking for someone to go out drinking with him and had wept on the phone as he told him about breaking up with Hope. Misery is calling now, he says, to see how Hope is. "It's presumptuous of me, I know," he tells her, "but I'd like it if you'd think of me as *your* friend, too."

Hope is both startled and touched. She thanks him and writes his number down, as he insists. He offers to take her to dinner sometime when she's feeling up to it.

A week later, he calls her again, renews his offer to take her to dinner, and suggests an evening two days hence. She accepts (although *she* ends up buying dinner; he supports himself on his assistantship, and after listening to him as he tells her about his life she realizes that he cannot possibly afford to pay for dinner for the two of them).

Besides exchanging thumbnail sketches of their day-to-day activities (he makes her laugh when he swears that he writes and reads philosophy *and* gets his teaching duties done in a grand total of four hours a day, and then spends every other waking minute watching television, drinking beer, and smoking cigarettes), and telling one another their life stories (briskly summarized, and heavy on their earliest, failed efforts at romance, in junior high and high school), they talk for a long time over dinner about her work and about Spinoza. Hope is moved inexplicably when Misery, in passing, mentions that Spinoza thought a virtuous man acted understanding *why* he had to, while all other men acted because they couldn't help themselves.

They get together twice more in the next month, once for lunch and once for dinner. She buys. He tells her jokes, and what's been happening on *Oprah*; he tells her in some detail the plots of reruns of old shows on cable—*Dick Van Dyke, Green Acres, Dobie Gillis*—and with hardly a breath in between he talks to her about innate ideas versus ideas derived from one's experience.

She talks mainly about Heartache, and when she does he just listens, for which she is grateful. She tells Misery she can't make herself stop thinking about how Heartache had ceased, out of the blue, to love her. How could that happen? she says. How can you love someone and then *not*? All Misery says then, after a long and thoughtful pause, is: "Don't you just hate rhetorical questions?" Hope talks about how she can't sleep since Heartache moved out; she talks about the empty places on the bookshelves—how she can't bring herself to push her own books over to close up the gaps; once, while talking, she begins to cry. Misery looks uncomfortable. Then she recovers and starts worrying aloud about how she can't keep on living in the loft alone—she can't afford it without Heartache—and about how she can't just throw out her subletter and move back to her old place—which (she's talking very fast now) would be depressing anyway—and about how just the thought of looking for a new place makes her want to crawl into a hole. She tries out on him an idea she's been playing with, of leaving New York altogether, maybe looking for a good job somewhere else. He says, "Why not? Why shouldn't you?" and she's relieved; she had imagined people saying, "How could you? Why *would* you? Are you nuts?" But Misery says, "Sounds good to me. I myself would love to get out of this city."

When a job offer comes (the director of a new "arts center" in the midwest used to live with someone who now lives with the ex-brother-in-law of Hope's old boss in SoHo, whom Hope by chance runs into on the very day he hears about the job—thus managing to get her application in *and* be flown out for an interview even before the job is advertised in the CAA newsletter), and Hope has to decide whether she should take it, it's Misery she calls, on impulse, for advice. He tells her she should take the job. "No question," he says. "Best thing for you—leave Heartache behind and get out of this godforsaken city. *Go*. I know you won't be sorry." But then he adds, "Of course, *I* will be."

　　She has dinner with him once more before she leaves town (this time, for the first time, he pays—he insists), and when afterwards he walks her home, he takes her hand—this too for the first time. And then he kisses her—once, chastely—when they say goodbye. And suddenly (it seems quite sudden, to her) Hope is living in a mid-sized middle western city, working at a brand new, university-owned Center for Contemporary Arts, where she is officially "Director of Exhibit Installation and Art Reclamation, Restoration, Rectification and Repair." What she *does*, for the most part, with the help of two part-timers and two student interns, is install and clean and undo minor harms inflicted by transit or storage. There *is* no restoration to be done here. Not only is the art so new there's nothing to restore, but more often than not—so she is told by the director—the artists whose work is exhibited *want* their work to deteriorate: "For them, you see, this is intrinsic to the process." Hope doesn't see, but she nods, smiles, and thinks that it is just as well—that at this point in her life she's glad to have a job that's practical and clear-cut: that has her cleaning things up, putting them into the galleries, and fixing them when they are broken. And it is a very good job. Her salary is generous; she has health insurance for the first time (she even has a life insurance policy—and she is flummoxed, briefly, when she's asked to name a beneficiary; she settles on her younger brother's youngest child). It's a straight nine-to-five affair,

Monday through Friday. Every night and on the weekends she can paint—and she has a fine studio now, separate from the large (and, by New York standards, dirt cheap) apartment that she lives in; both are walking distance from the campus. She asks herself, quite seriously—challenging herself—what else she possibly could need. She doesn't let herself reflect on Heartache; she sends him a change of address card, the official-looking kind you get from the post office, but across the bottom she writes *FYI, for emergencies only.* Then she underlines *only.* Then she underlines *emergencies.* For now she is too busy to consider being lonely.

Misery writes to her. He is finishing his dissertation—getting close, he says—and looking for a teaching job, having no luck finding one; he'll probably be on the street soon, he says, pushing all his books and papers in a shopping cart. He tells her what he has been reading lately, criticizes it ferociously, reports on how many "oh, Rob's" there were in that day's episode of *Dick Van Dyke*, and writes out every joke he's heard since Hope left town. Hope writes back, charmed. Soon they are writing to each other regularly. His letters fascinate her. He is pessimistic about everything, but he makes jokes about it. Hope thinks he's the wittiest *and* the most cynical man she has ever met. She takes an optimistic tone in her letters to him. She lists reasons that he might consider being happier. He writes back with a numbered list of two hundred and fourteen reasons not to be. His list makes her laugh. But she can tell, too, that he's serious, in his way: he really does see the world as a grim place. This has a curious effect on her: it both attracts and dismays her. She finds herself writing about life's pleasures, goodness, beauty—about purposefulness, meaning, and redemption. In response, he mocks her gently; he addresses her as Hopeless.

She writes to him about her job. She has become "a little bit obsessed," she tells him, with the idea that some artists *want* what they have made to fall apart. *Maybe I don't have enough to do,* she writes, *or I'm just easily distracted, but I find that I keep thinking: Why do it if you don't want it to last? I want my little landscapes to outlast me—I want them to be around forever. (Do you think this is a bourgeois attitude?)*

Misery responds that it seems "just right" to him for an artist to *want* works of art to "last eternally." *But you can't* know *they will, can you?* he writes. *It's the uncertainty that interests me. I wonder if it—the uncertainty—wouldn't have some effect on your 'process' (as they say). Are you consciously aware, as you work on a painting, that it may fall into ruin over time despite all your best efforts?*

She thinks this over. She doesn't know the answer—she has no idea what she is thinking as she works, she tells him (it feels like a confession)—but she doesn't mind *considering* it. She is struck by the difference between his questions and Heartache's. Misery is so *respectful* of her. He asks her to send him slides of her paintings, and when she does he writes back with comments that are smart, perceptive, helpful to her, and entirely positive. Unlike Heartache, Misery does not find it disturbing that she paints from her imagination. *He* thinks it is interesting; he asks if she's always worked this way, and she tells him about how, in her first art classes when she was an undergraduate, forced to draw and paint from life, she'd hated it—how even as an exercise it made her fidgety, uneasy. And because he doesn't ask her why, she volunteers in her next letter that she thinks it may just be a matter of attention: it's hard for her to pay attention to how things *are*, really; she'd prefer to concentrate on what she is imagining.

Their letters become longer and more frequent. Hope looks forward to his; she hurries home from work to see if that day's mail has brought one. They are writing very often now—they are up to three, and sometimes four, letters a week—letters of six, seven pages. By this time they have told each other nearly everything about themselves. They know enough about each other's day-to-day lives that she can name all his friends

and even the two best and three worst students in the class
he's teaching this term, and talk knowledgeably of the "numerous peculiarities" of his advisors, and the "whimsical and
contradictory" demands they make concerning what must be
the fifth or sixth draft of his dissertation. *He* by now knows
more about the habits of the various eccentrics working at the
arts center than do most people *at* the university; he knows
exactly how her studio is laid out (she has, at his request, sent
him a snapshot); he knows what kinds of food she likes best
when she's feeling sad (cream of wheat, tomato soup, canned
peaches, and macaroni with hot milk and butter); he knows
how much she loved the Betsy-Tacy books when she was growing up; he knows that she reads novels at night just before she
goes to sleep, and that she will read *all* the novels of a single
author before she goes on to someone else—and he knows
whose novels it is she is reading now (Paul Auster's) and whose
she plans to read next (George Eliot's—though she's decided
in advance not to read both *Romola* and *Felix Holt*, but to choose
one of these; she has a set of loopholes she allows herself—
which Misery now knows about—including also the elimina-
tion of first novels, if it turns out they are very bad); he knows
that Henry Jaglom is her favorite film director.

     He tells her about Eliot's translations of Spinoza—
had she known about them? he asks (she had not)—and explains rationalism, describes Spinoza's theory of truth, and
tells her about techniques for verifying what one "knows."
She tells *him*, step by step, how to make an oil painting archi-
val—"or, as *you'd* say, how to *try* to (or pretend to?), knowing
full well it just might not work." She tells him that the term
used by conservators for the materials used in a painting that
are bound to fail is "the inherent vice"—and that, because of
its inherent vice, "The Last Supper" was a ruin within fifty
years ("What *I* wonder," she says, "is if there's anyone who'd
claim that this was purposeful on Leonardo's part—more evidence of genius: proof that he believed art *shouldn't* outlast

life—and not an accident, a truly awful accident, as a result of
his experimental methods").

They exchange dreams. He sends her his recipe for
chili; she sends him her recipes for lentil soup and guacamole.
He explains "semantic paradoxes" (the example he gives her
is of "a young man saying to his date: 1) *Will you answer this
question in the same way that you will answer the next one? 2) Will
you sleep with me?*"—and points out that unless she lies, the
woman's answer to the second question must be yes. "This is
a favorite of my intro logic class," he tells her). She tells him
about the painter Albert Pinkham Ryder, who painted without waiting for the underpainting he had done to dry, and who
mixed wax and oil "and *all* sorts of non-archival materials—
experimenting with whatever struck his fancy at the moment"—and who seemed not to *care* what happened to his
paintings ("I suppose you could say *he* was liberated both from
the compulsion to preserve *and* from some kind of 'conviction' that it's wrong for art to last"). What troubles her about
him is that many of his paintings were completely changed by
"restoration"—colors altered, figures wiped out. "So it's not
as if they didn't last—they're around, all right—but they've
been 'restored' to a state that never *was*. Talk about semantic
paradoxes," Hope says.

Misery says there's something he has to tell her—something he feels he "must just come out and say," although he is
afraid that Hope will think he's lost his mind. He thinks—no,
in fact, he is sure—that he's in love with her. He says he knows
that it sounds "a little crazy," that she needn't remind him that
they've seen each other only a few times. *I know, I know, I know,*
he says. *But still, this is the way I feel.* He says it seems to him
he knows her better than he has ever known anyone—that they
have come to understand each other far more deeply this way
than they could have in "the ordinary ways." *Don't you think
this is true?* he asks her. *Don't you think we know each other better
than most people* ever *do?*

She does think so. The word *love* comes as something
of a shock—but not, she finds upon reflection, as a *bad* shock;
no, it isn't unpleasant in the least to read that sentence (which
she rereads many, *many* times before she forces herself to set
down the letter—and then cannot keep from picking it up once
again): *I think—no, in fact, I am sure—that I'm in love with you.*
Indeed, after she has spent perhaps a half-hour sitting at her
kitchen table, with the letter at first in her hand, then face down
on the table—then in her hand again, then folded and back in
the envelope, then out again and back in her hand—she finds
she is thinking: *Well, yes, of course, that's it. Obviously.* That's
what this has been—love.

And now this becomes the subject of their letters. They
discuss love endlessly—they discuss love with the same ear-
nestness and interest with which they had been discussing art,
philosophy, food, books, and people. It seems to take no time
before it has become a simple, as if long-accepted *fact:* they
love each other. Of course they do! Why had it taken them so
long to see it? They demand of one another. They both close
their letters now with the phrase "Missing you severely" (he
had been the first to use it; she had followed, and it had become the standard)—which strikes her as odd (she still has
this much distance from the matter): *Can* they miss each other
if they've hardly ever been in the same room together? And
yet—oh, and yet! she thinks—it truly feels as if they do. *She*
feels it; she is wrenched by longing. She reads each of his letters again and again—they're much shorter now, sometimes
only half a page—until she knows it by heart. *What will become
of us?* he asks her, more than once. *How will we manage this?*
She repeats these lines to herself as she walks to and from work,
to and from the studio.

Caught up in the romance, Hope doesn't stop to think.
The director of the arts center is a good friend of the dean of
the college of fine arts; the dean, Hope knows—they have been
frequent guests at the same dinner parties—lives with the chair

of the philosophy department. Hope takes a deep breath and one day before she goes to lunch she pokes her head into the office of the director and asks for "some advice" in what she calls only a "personal matter"—testing first to see if this alarms her boss—and when she finds that there is not only no hint of alarm or anxiety on the director's pleasant middle western face, but rather a look of delight (a stroke of luck, she thinks—for it is Hope's conviction that there are two kinds of people in the world, those who dread being asked for favors and those who are thrilled by it, and there was no telling until now which kind her boss might turn out to be), she slips all the way into the office, sits down on the edge of the postmodern récamier across from the director's huge, transparent desk, and wonders aloud whether there would be a way to secure "something—anything at all"—in the philosophy department for "this man I'm sort of seeing," she says (she does not—cannot—say that she has hardly *seen* the man at all). And it seems that the director is not just the helpful sort but a romantic, too, and within minutes, on the telephone, plans have been made for brunch that Sunday for all those concerned—director, dean, chair, Hope. The brunch goes well. It goes so well that Misery, that very week, receives a phone call offering him a one-year lecturing appointment starting in the fall.

Misery, who has run out of years on his assistantship, and had all but resigned himself to unemployment in the fall (for by now it is late July, and all the jobs he tried for have been filled), is flabbergasted. Hope discovers that she is embarrassed. She reminds him it's not *that* good a job (no benefits, low salary, six sections of the same course—Introduction to Philosophy for Non-Majors—each one with fifty students) and it's not renewable. Misery assures her that it's better than a lot of jobs he *has* applied for and for which he has been turned down. Their letters now are all about this: about the job, his gratitude and his amazement, Hope's embarrassment, and finally—as the midpoint of August is approaching—their plans for the year. They will be sensible, they say: he'll come out the first weekend of September, and he won't *live* with Hope—he will merely "stay with her" until he gets a paycheck; then he'll find his own apartment. The main thing, they tell each other, is that now they'll have a chance to get to know each other "in the ordinary way." They can see how things develop between them, and Misery can get his dissertation done while working at this job and looking for another. If all goes well—if he gets a tenure-track job somewhere *and* they are happy together— they'll decide then what to do. In the meantime, Hope tells herself, what is there to be so nervous about? She reminds herself that they have been getting to know each other slowly— that she hasn't rushed into this, even if it looks that way. They know each other very well; they know things about each other no one *else* knows about either of them; it's unlikely that there will be too many surprises.

Misery rolls into town on Labor Day, driving a U-Haul. Hope helps him to unload and carry into her apartment a rolled-up twin-sized futon; a TV; a beat-up IBM Selectric type- writer; a chipped red metal folding chair; a hollow wooden door marked by a set of interlocking coffee cup rings, ink stains, scratches, and a zigzag trail of cigarette burns; two stunningly heavy, battered, gray two-drawer file cabinets; twelve boxes of "books/philosophy" and thirty-some-odd (she thinks; she stops counting when she reaches twenty-eight) of "books/ miscellaneous"; three boxes marked "clothes, pens, pencils, paper, shoes, notebooks, &c"; and one unmarked, untaped, and to all appearances completely randomly packed box that Hope (at a loss now that everything has been brought in and she and Misery, with nothing more to do, are all alone and sweaty in her living room) begins to rummage through. She isn't sure— she can't bring herself to look directly at him—but she *thinks* he is smiling as he watches, sprawled on her Goodwill couch, his feet resting on a box of books/philosophy, and since she doesn't know what else to do she just keeps digging through the box, naming aloud what each thing she comes across is: a high-intensity desk lamp, a softball, a clock radio, a hammer, a church key, an iron skillet, a red lava lamp, and a can opener— this last item the one she still has in her hand when Misery comes to her, puts his arms around her with a sigh, and draws her across the room, back to the couch; and then they're *on* the couch together, and then—somehow—on the floor, in the narrow channel in between the couch and all the rows of boxes—and Hope feels as if she's holding her breath the en- tire time (although surely she *can't* be, she thinks; wouldn't she die?), and everything about this seems improbable—and so perplexing she can't really *think* at all—and afterwards, as she lies still on the rough carpeting that came with the apart- ment, her eyes closed, her head turned sideways so her fore- head touches the square leg of the Goodwill couch she had bought the day *she* had arrived in town, and tries to figure out how she feels beyond simply overwhelmed, Misery says maybe she should sit up; he has to say something that he might as well get out of the way now—he'd thought it could wait a few days but he feels "too weird about it" to keep it a secret any longer. He has met someone else, in New York; he be- lieves he is in love with *her*.

It is at this point that Hope has what used to be called— there seems to be no satisfactory phrase for it anymore—a ner- vous breakdown.

But first things first: she has to get Misery and all his boxes out of her apartment. She does this calmly the next day. She calls in sick and goes out for the morning paper, and with- out a word to *him* (though he keeps trying to get her to talk to him; he keeps trying to explain: he tells her that he met this other woman just over a week ago; he didn't mean for this to happen; he feels terrible about it; how could he have known that such a thing would happen?), she studies the apartments- for-rent ads and then makes the necessary phone calls; she even lends him money to pay his first month's rent and security—

she even gives him a few things she doesn't absolutely need (a window fan, her extra cutting board, a knife, a loaf of bread, a bag of sugar, and a box of salt). And only after she has once more helped him with his boxes, desk-top door, file cabinets, chair, TV, futon, and typewriter, does she take to her bed and stay there.

It's not a choice she makes—it's not as if she chooses to give up. She *doesn't* give up. She just gives out. That's how she feels. She feels that there is nothing left: she is exhausted.

The phone rings every few hours on the first day, and she doesn't answer it; then, on the second day, it rings so often, and keeps ringing for so long each time, she pulls the plug. By the next Monday morning, when the arts center's director comes to the apartment, banging on the door and yelling, "Hope? Hope, if you're in there, dammit, open up!", she hasn't said a word or eaten anything—she hasn't risen from the bed at all except for rare trips to the bathroom—for five days.

It's not a long breakdown, or "psychic smash-up"— which is what the director calls it while persuading her to check into the hospital ("It's not that big a deal—trust me, I know. I've done it twice myself")—or "difficult time" (what she tells her parents, on the phone), or "clinical depression" (what they tell her in the hospital): she's back in her apartment in less than three weeks, and she returns to work almost immediately (if she doesn't, she knows, she may drift back into bed). At the arts center, people speak to her in just above a whisper, hug her carefully and bring her cups of herbal tea; they lightly touch her arm at the day's end and tell her to "take care," emphasizing *care* so that she'll know it isn't just a pleasantry. They treat her as if she were breakable—and for some time after she gets out of the hospital, she feels as if she *is*. But it's not only that she feels she has turned fragile; she feels smaller, too—she feels as if there is now *less* of her.

This is what she means when she says now that they— Heartache and Misery—"changed" her. She means they wore her down and left less of her in the end than there had been before. It had seemed to her at first that they hadn't left *anything*. But she was wrong. If she had been right, she never would have gotten out of bed. What's left, she thinks, is delicate and unprotectable, and yet still *her*; she endures.

But is this "change"—the kind of change that's meant when we say that "to be a story, there must be a change in the main character"? It's possible Hope hasn't changed at all, but only thinks she has.

And that this "story" isn't one at all, but only thinks it is.

I feel obliged to mention this, because it's almost over now—there's really very little left to tell—and I can see I've been remiss in many ways. I've told almost the whole story in summary—rushed through months (*years*) of Hope's life at breakneck speed, with hardly any dialogue, the barest hint of "setting," and no background on the characters (who *are* these people, anyway? Where are they from? Who are their parents? At the very least I could have told you what Hope, Misery, and Heartache *look* like)—but there doesn't seem to be much point in slowing down now. It's too late; the story's gone on long enough. At this stage, the niceties of storytelling might as *well* be set aside. And I can't see the sense in taking pains *now* to make sure that I "show/don't tell" you something that you'll find (so I imagine; *I* do) quite astonishing: that Hope, just two years after the last of the events described herein, considers both Heartache and Misery her "friends."

Misery is still in town, though unemployed: the job Hope managed to get for him ended, as expected, in June of last year. He stays, he says, because he has no money for another move, and has nowhere to go in any case—he says New York is now impossible, financially. (Hope has her own ideas about his failure to return to New York. He still has that "girlfriend" there—the one he met the week before he left the city—and for two years they have been corresponding. He gets by, just barely, with proofreading and the occasional translation, while he looks for a "real job" for next year, somewhere else. He has at last finished his dissertation, and this past May he took the bus to New York to defend it; his diploma came in the mail not two weeks ago (Hope cooked dinner for him that night—nothing fancy, just spaghetti—to help celebrate).

Heartache too has graduated, finally, and he too is now looking for a tenure-track job. He and Hope have been in touch again since he happened to call, for the first time since she had left New York ("It begins to seem to me, Hope, that the passage of so much time in itself constitutes an emergency"), soon after her stay in the hospital. He'd had no idea about that, and he cried when she told him. It wasn't until then that he learned of her correspondence-romance with his old friend Misery. "Oh, *no*," he kept saying as she told him the story. "Oh, *no*. Hope! Jesus *Christ*"—so that she thought he was angry with *her*, for getting involved with Misery in the first place, but after a few minutes it emerged that it was *Misery* he was so furious at. "How could he? How *could* he?" he said—and Hope couldn't tell if he meant "how could he have put the moves on *you*?" or "how could he have two-timed you and dumped you?" She decided not to ask. But when, much later—over a year later, when he calls to tell her that he is in love and thinking about getting married—Hope mentions that she has had dinner recently with Misery, he is enraged: he tells her he can't understand how she can "still be friends with that guy after all he put you through." Hope laughs; she tells him she ends up on friendly terms with all of her ex-boyfriends. Heartache says—he says it without any irony—he can't see how or why she does it. And Hope says, "But that's just how I am."

And so it is. That's Hope. Wouldn't *you* think, after all this, that she would not only have nothing to do with Misery and Heartache, but that she'd be tempted to give up on men and on love altogether? But no: two years after Misery, she is in love again. It's true. She is in love with a man I won't

name because he isn't *in* this story—that's another story altogether, a much happier, more hopeful one (it will be called—
I'll gladly tell you this much—"Hope and Pray"). That's Hope
for you: she's in love, she's happy, and she's on congenial terms
with Misery and Heartache.

These days she and Heartache talk on the phone regularly—twice a month or so. He calls her for pep talks, sympathy, and (he reminds her) "good old conversation—we always
had that, didn't we?" His girlfriend, a young photographer,
has left him. "It's my karma, isn't it?" he asks Hope. He sighs,
and Hope is silent. The question doesn't seem to require a
real answer.

She sees Misery about as often as she talks to Heartache. She cooks dinner for him, since he can't afford meals
out, and she won't pay for him in restaurants (that's the upper
limit, she tells him, of her indulgence). He brings the latest
copy of *Jobs for Philosophers* when he comes over, and after dinner he sits in her one good chair—she bought it new, this summer—with an ashtray balanced on one knee and a beer can on
the other, shaking his head, muttering, "Moscow, Idaho. Au-
gusta, Georgia. Middle-of-nowhere-*damn*-cold, Michigan,"
and, "One-year term appointment, non-renewable, non-ten-
ure track, no health benefits, twelve thousand dollars, twelve
classes a semester, also do the chairman's laundry."

Hope laughs, as she is meant to.

He is visiting her now—*right* now, as we speak. We
shall look in on them. Perhaps it will tell us something that
will help us understand Hope.

There he is, in the good chair; it is a chintz-covered
wing chair. Hope is on the Goodwill couch she still has not
replaced, although she can afford to. Misery is making gloomy
jokes about his unemployability, and Hope is saying serious
and cheerful things, insisting that he'll find something that's
worthy of him if he just keeps looking. She feels now, as she
often does when she is with him, that it is her *job* to give him

reasons to be optimistic. She sometimes thinks that without knowing it *that* had been why she'd fallen for him—*because* she had to be so optimistic for his sake. Hope liked herself best when she was most optimistic. Even now she has the vague idea that if she can convince *him* that life is good, she will have convinced herself—that in fact it will simply be true.

Heartache's problem, on the other hand, she thinks, was that he couldn't understand why life was *ever* less than utterly good. He wanted—he expected—to be happy every moment. It was the only thing that counted for him: trying to be happy.

Hope is thinking about both of them as she sits in her living room with Misery, who has now fallen silent. He is drinking, smoking, looking grim. Hope tries to think of something to say that will interest or amuse him. The best thing, she knows, would be a joke, but all the jokes she knows are those that *he* has told her. She decides at last to tell him about Andrea Mantegna, the Renaissance painter. She has been reading about him, and thinking of making a trip to New York to see a show of his paintings at the Met. She tells Misery about how he used animal glue instead of egg as the medium for his paintings, and left them unvarnished—and about the brilliance and fragility of the work as a result of this; about how the layers of varnish applied later by the owners of the paintings not only destroyed their character but darkened them and muddied them—so that even the most glorious scenes of redemption seem to be *about* gloom and unhappiness.

But as she talks, *she* begins to feel depressed. Not about Mantegna's paintings, but because there was a time when telling Misery about such things, in letters, gave her so much pleasure—and seemed to give *him* such pleasure, too. And now, she can see for herself, he isn't listening to her. He doesn't care. She knows that—and yet she can't stop. She *won't* stop. She won't give up; she *can't*—Hope can't stop talking.

And this is where, I am afraid, I must leave her. I can't

stay at her side forever—obviously not. She'll go on without me—without *us*, watching her. She was there before this story started, and she'll be there long after we've left her. There's nothing else I can do with her, really, but what I have done: set her down here, let you get to know her. And you do now. Trust me: what I've told you about Hope is all you *need* to know.

I have an idea about what you might *want* to know. I suspect you want to know who *I* am. And why wouldn't you? Why should you believe a word I say, when you don't even know me?

Well, because you have no choice. Who else should you believe? Who else *is* there? I'm the only one here—it's my voice in your ear. You'll have to trust me, or trust nobody. Without me, there would *be* no Hope—and there would be no Heartache and no Misery. There would be nothing.

Don't wait for any more. That's it—that's the end. That's the whole story.